RECEIVED

JUL 28 2018

Douglass-Truth Branch Library

Starfire
A Red Peace

NO LONGER PROPERTY OF
SEATTLE PUBLIC LIBRARY

D1014391

NO LONGER PROPERTY OF

RECEIVED

NOV 1 7 2017

Douglass-Truth Branch Library

STARFIRE

A RED PEACE

SPENCER ELLSWORTH

A TOM DOHERTY ASSOCIATES BOOK

NEW YORK

This is a work of fiction. All of the characters, organizations, and events portrayed in this novella are either products of the author's imagination or are used fictitiously.

STARFIRE: A RED PEACE

Copyright © 2017 by Spencer Ellsworth

All rights reserved.

Cover art by Sparth
Cover design by Christine Foltzer

Edited by Beth Meacham

A Tor.com Book
Published by Tom Doherty Associates
175 Fifth Avenue
New York, NY 10010

www.tor.com

Tor® is a registered trademark of
Macmillan Publishing Company, LLC.

ISBN 978-0-7653-9572-6 (ebook)
ISBN 978-0-7653-9573-3 (trade paperback)

First Edition: August 2017

To Dad & Chrissy,
who inspired, cajoled, listened, brainstormed,
and most important, read.

The blood stars, the bleeding galaxy, spin in their orbits, wounds open to the cold, and only the cold cauterizes. The warlord burns the suns out, stepping from one to the other. The son of the stars faces the giants who stride the worlds, and he is armed but with faith . . .

—Third Book of Joria

Overture

THE PLANET IRITHESSA was rank with the memory of war.

In orbit, the shattered warships floated. Clouds of dead things formed tendrils between the wreckage. Dead circuits, wires, and paneling streaming silver in the sunlight, dead bodies, veins and tendons exposed, cold eyes open against the too-bright sun of orbit. For them, there had been one moment of flashing, scouring fire, and now eternal cold.

War had frozen hope, fear, love, on ten thousand worlds all over the galaxy, for ten years.

At last, it was over.

On the surface of the planet, smoke rose over the crystal pyramids of the capital city, drifted through the leaves of the famous gardens, but there was no roar of shard-fire in the streets, no clatter of soulswords. In the distance, the mountains lit up with flashes of red and the thunder of shards, but as each hour passed, the sound faded, before the soft whistle of the evening wind.

In the main square, the emperor's body swung in the breeze, hanged from the statue of his predecessor. The body was a husk, gray and empty-eyed.

In the Imperial Tower, one man stood, dark against the glowing, swirling map of the galaxy. Like all his troops, he'd been grown in a vat, yanked out slimy and febrile by mechanized arms, given a data dump to serve as his memories, given a number without a name, and loaded onto a drop ship to be another casualty in an unwinnable war. They had called them cannon fodder. Ugly, but necessary. Not really sentient. Now, the name he had chosen was on every communiqué across a thousand worlds. John Starfire, who had taken the half-human cross soldiers and formed an army against corrupt human royalty.

His beard had gone half silver, his green eyes lined with wrinkles. As he stared at the map, he removed his battle helmet, the silver shining in the faint light. He put a hand to his great soulsword. His hand twitched on the blade, then calmed.

He had freed the galaxy. He had made peace with the Dark Zone, and eradicated the old royalty. He was finally able to rest.

But fear crawled across those worn features. He clutched his sword hilt again, so tightly his hand turned bloodless white.

"Sir?" came a voice from the entrance to the room. "You've been in here a long time. We found more Imperial officers. What . . . what do we do with them?"

He turned, and faced three of his Vanguard, and his wife.

"We've been fighting so long," he said, his voice soft and ragged. "Can we fight as long as it takes?"

They shifted. His wife met his eyes, her pale, tired face lit by the blue light of the star map. He took a few steps forward, put his hand on her shoulder.

"I thought you would finally sleep," she said.

"I'm thinking," he said. "I think we can finally do it."

"Do it?" His Vanguard looked between themselves, clearly wondering what was left to do.

"You know the order," he said.

"*The* order?" one of them asked.

"Directive zero."

They stared back blankly.

"It's time," he said, "to kill every human in this galaxy."

1

Jaqi

OKAY, SO I AM in a fighting pit. With a very big, very tattooed, and three-horned Zarra who is actually licking blood off his hands. Oh, it's alien blood, but still the stuff of life. Close enough to the stuff in my half-breed veins.

All because of tomatoes.

Let me back up. My name's Jaqi, and I'm some human, some Jorian. In space, among the wild worlds, that means good food is hard to find.

See, I've been on a cricket ship, flying dark nodes for the last year. The crickets' ship smells and is cramped and built for exoskeletons, not arms and legs, but they pay top dollar for my talents. No, the problem with being in the wild for months at a time is the food. It's not long before the fresh supplies are gone and you're rehydrating squares of protein. Peanut butter–flavored protein, chocolate-flavored protein, thurkuk-secretion-flavored protein (that one actually tastes more like peanut butter than the peanut butter–flavored one).

After a month, you want to puke every time you see a little brown cube. I even tried the captain's meal-loam. It's just not fair that a cricket's food stores better than a humanoid's. I threw it up, which is standard in space, but they laughed at me too, that weird cricket noise where the bristles on their backs scrape together, and then I had to put up with that for the rest of the year.

Screech, screech, scratch. Protein cube, protein cube.

So the minute we touched down in Real Live People Space, as opposed to the wild where we'd been doing shady deals for the last year, I went looking for Real Live People Food. Specifically tomatoes.

The best, of course, are the kind my mother used to give me in our tenant worker days. My parents brought home the ones that split along the top. The growers couldn't sell them so marred.

My mother would cut one and sprinkle salt on it, while she sang the field songs, tapping her hips against the kitchen counter. She'd give me the slice, and each time, it tasted like sunlight.

Today, I would settle for half-ripe orbital hothouse tomatoes with yeast flakes. And maybe a nice boy, who doesn't mind a one-day romance. Or a girl. Or someone don't fit either, long as they're looking for a time. I'm not picky.

Orbital Ecosphere 912 is a nice place, for a bug-crawling pen of the galaxy's swine. I'm not being high-headed—the locals call it Swiney Niney. All the environmental controls are stuck, so the place sits at a swampy 110 percent humidity. It smells like rotting food—actually, the air is so thick that it really tastes like rotting food. Swiney, slimy, grimy Niney.

I just finished my contract with the crickets, and I got about four hours to play before I need to track down real work. I'm going to make the most of it.

The signs flash at me when we debark, probably important. Yeah, I can't read. Who cares? My mother was teaching me, but she didn't know much either. She vanished when I was eight, and after that there was nothing to do but work, on any ship that would take me. I can read nav charts, them with the numbers and lines, but all those letters go fuzzy when they sit in a row. It would be nice to read, with all those hours in the wild, but I somehow manage not to go crazy.

One day I'll learn. When it's safe for me to come into mid-galaxy.

In Swiney Niney's main square, there's usually a bustling market. Full of food. Now . . . just a few stalls, selling cloth that looks like it needs ironing, and maybe some stain-work. A food stall, but they're just selling high-grade protein. And not much else. Most of the market is missing.

I've had nightmares like this.

Folks hurry by, but they have their heads down, staring at their rapidly moving feet. There is a new stain—blood?—in the middle of the square. Everyone seems to be headed for high ground. A long time ago, this ecosphere was 10 percent trading post, 90 percent park, and now the park has turned into a trackless wilderness, good for hiding. And it seems like everyone's gone hiding.

The only guy at peace is the skull-faced, tattooed Necro priest, shaking his staff in the air and creaking, "Death!" Those guys only know one word. As long as they're shouting it, they're happy.

"Hey," I say to one of the scabs running by. "Hey, what's going on? Where's the food?"

He darts away, even faster.

"*Skrit*," I yell at some kind of sentient bug I don't recognize. I hope the crickets' language—at least the human pidgin version of it, minus the screeching hairs on the back—will work. "*Skrit secca nee?*"

It squeaks along on its way. Nothing.

"Looking for answers?"

The guy has come up behind me silently. He's a sight. I am in a tank top and shorts and wish I could go naked in the Swiney Niney heat, but he wears a black trench coat and a wide-brimmed hat over a beard. He manages to look at me from under that hat without letting me see his eyes.

Con man. Screaming con man.

"Salutes," I say. "Answers without a price tag."

He laughs. "I like you. Why en't you reading the screens?"

That's embarrassing. "Bad eyes," I say. Common enough excuse.

"The Resistance won. Irithessa has fallen."

"Oh."

That takes a minute.

"Oh!"

There's a good reason why we were tenant farmers, see. My folks were both vat-grown, the most common cross—70 percent human DNA, 30 percent Jorian—and both pronounced defective. They were supposed to go back in the vats, be boiled down for spares, but they escaped.

They didn't join the Resistance, like other crosses did; they kept their heads down, and I did too. But we sure hoped for the Resistance. Everyone loves the Resistance—human, cricket, cross, gasbag—everyone. I saw pictures of the leader, John Starfire. He's the greatest soulsword-swinger in the galaxy, and handsome. Gets my girl blood going. Everyone except the blue-bloods wants an end to the war, to shortage of rations and restrictions on travel, not to mention all the Imperial crosses getting vat-cooked up just to die in the Dark Zone.

Not want to. They have.

The galaxy *is* free.

I can learn to read.

I can go to school. I can get married and have kids. I can buy alcohol!

The con man seems to be reading my stupefied face fairly well. "You're a cross?"

"No," I say, instantly on guard. "Pure human."

"That's too bad," he says. "Real evil shame, that. I could use a cross right now who wanted to make some money. You know, ever since Irithessa fell, the Imperial nodes en't worth a damn. Supplies backed up or gone, but I might know where some real matter is stowed away."

It must be the euphoria. Or the hunger. My instincts are telling me that this guy is as tricky as a bad node. I don't listen to them, fool me. "I might have some Jorian in me. For real matter."

"Hot meal," he says. "You just have to earn it." He turns and starts walking off, that trench coat swaying. Even that looks like a con. Or so I would think. Any other time.

"I'll do it," I say.

And that's how I get to the fighting pit.

Oh, first he has a couple big Rorgs take my knives and toss me into a cage. Not just any cage—they've decorated the place with a carpet of centipedes. Big centipedes. There's a billion varieties of centipede in the galaxy, and they all give me the shivers.

"What is this?" I ask, as I climb the sides of the cage.

"This is what you do to earn that hot meal," he sneers. "My name's Cade. You do right for me and I'll reward you."

"What are you—" I squirm, trying to keep both my legs hooked around the top of the cage. The nearest Rorg whacks my leg with a stick. "I'm going to kill you!"

"Let 'em bite you," Cade says. "Those centipedes are specially made for the pits. The venom will make you faster. Stronger."

"I'll rip off your—" I use every curse in human or cricket or trader's slang I know. He smiles a big, nasty smile from under that stupid hat, and closes the hatch, leaving me there in the dark with the centipedes, a squirming glistening mass below me.

Centipedes, aiya. All of them are straight from the Dark Zone, I swear. Even the sentient ones.

Of course, I get distracted from centipedes when the door to the side of me opens, and reveals a big pit dug into the roots of a half-dozen giant trees. A seven-foot Zarra, all tattoos and big horns, is fighting a smaller, scaly little Sska. It slinks around the edges of the pit and hisses at the Zarra, but he en't five suns within intimidated. He goes crazing and charges right into the burning saliva, getting welts on his skin, and catches the Sska by its shoulder and rips it in half. Just rips it in half, like he's cutting his meat.

That's when they shunt my cage into the pit, and tip it over. What was the top flies open, which means I crawl out just ahead of the centipedes.

The ground here's been mixed to mud. Blood mud, I reckon. The pit started as a pleasant natural hollow, sunk in the center of a ring of big old trees. The thick roots have grown into natural ring-side seats for the scabs looking down on us. A cheap plasticized barrier runs around the rim of the pit, and all the swine of Swiney Niney are sitting above or on the top of the barrier.

The Zarra licks the Sska's blood off his hands and looks at me.

Cade yells old-fashioned style from his spot on one of the bigger tree branches.

"The talk of the hour! She is a real Jorian crossbreed, a killer, one of those who has conquered the galaxy, as of today, my friends! But can she conquer Zaragathora, Eater of Flesh?"

"Zaragathora?" I ask, looking at the Zarra. "Really?"

He snarls. A good snarl. Deep in the throat, rattling the lungs. This scab has practiced.

"I believe she can," he goes on.

Oh, by all Dark stars. He's got fighting Jorians on the brain. I don't have a soulsword, I en't never fought no dragons or thrown planets into the sun. What Jorian DNA lives in my cross body does exactly this: I can fly a ship. Specifically, I can enter faster-than-light, pure space, all on my lonesome, without a node-code. I'm a navigator.

Cade says, "She is a killer of the mind, and that is why we will make things a little more interesting. Creatures of worlds both wild and civilized, the NecroWasp!"

"The what?"

Opposite the Zarra, and just off my right side, a door opens in the side of the pit.

The thing coming out is just about the strangest cross I've ever seen. Insect head, working those mandibles. Big, pale, burly body, humanoid, with exoskeleton peeping through the skin. A mammoth stinger protruding from its belly. It smells like every dead thing in the universe got together and had a party.

You hear these things about fighting pits, but you don't think you'll go there. (Because you're sane, and you stay out of fighting pits! Unless you're too stupid to sense trouble.)

"Death!" I look up and see the Necro priest cheering on this thing. That explains it. Bits of dead things, crossed and brought back by Necros for joy. No doubt a favorite pet.

"Death!" the crowd roars with him.

Tomatoes.

The NecroWasp goes for the bigger target, Zaraga—let's just call him Z—and I run away from the whole business. I reach the plastic barrier and leap up, grab the top, and start to scramble over, but Cade draws a half shotgun and points it right at my head. "End it," he says.

Back into the pit.

The NecroWasp charges for Z, and Z looks a bit confused. Must be hard, realizing that he can't fight this thing with his usual head on, rip-its-arm-off method. He ducks away, darts toward me, and I dart away from both of them, duck and weave and duck and weave until I duck and weave myself right into the plastic barrier around the pit.

There are a lot of boos at our running, which makes old Z mad. He decides to charge the NecroWasp. It jabs that stinger out for him to skewer himself on. He changes his mind and dodges it, ducks again. The Wasp catches a claw in his skin, tears a gash along his head, and this time it's his own blood running into his face.

"Our cross is hanging back, folks. Should we try to persuade her?"

Cade actually fires! Shard-fire, from his shotgun. It plows up the ground at my feet, splatters mud on my face, sends red flames across the dirt. Trying to make me dance. I hold my ground. No promoter's going to shoot his prize.

Cade looks like he is trying to say something. It must be nasty, because it is stuck in his throat. And then it appears stuck in his brain, because his whole forehead is pulsing.

No, scratch that—someone has stuck him! A black blade jabs out of the front of his shirt, but that shirt stays dry as dust, and then the blade's gone. A flash of gray runs from him.

And then—well, then, I have to dodge the sun-sized mass of NecroWasp and Zarra dancing toward me. I run along the barrier, but one of those NecroWasp mandibles grabs me by the leg and slings me into the air, until I land in the mud. Something smacks me on the head—a rock or perhaps a Zarra foot.

I'm going to die, right as I got my freedom.

But no, my vision clears. I try to breathe and get a lungful of muddy water. I make my arms move, scrabble over the ground, force myself up, and I see Cade, lying dead in front of me where he's fallen into the pit.

I scramble to my feet and grab Cade's shotgun from his dead hand, coughing all the while. I turn around and shoot at the first one I see, which turns out to be the NecroWasp. The shard-fire blows off half its bug face. Doesn't stop it from coming for me. I shoot it ten more times in the face, until the charge goes. It takes a long time to fall over, and when it does, it hits the ground like a fifty-ton fighter wreck. The soupy mud shakes like it's going to suck me under.

The audience is running. Z takes a long, tattooed, and angry look at me, then Cade's body, and bellows the only words he's said so far. "Where is my money?"

I en't got any thoughts to answer him. I'm busy looking at Cade. Eyes red, skin gone gray, and for all that big old stab wound, not a drop of blood. I'd bet lost Earth that his memories just outlived his body.

This man has enemies, but on this day of all days, why is a dumb human con being stabbed, secret-like, by a Jorian soulsword?

2

Araskar

WINNING A WAR isn't the best feeling of my life, but it's up there.

My ears haven't stopped ringing, so I don't hear much of the speech. After planetfall, and after having a pyramid explode next to me, I doubt they'll ever stop ringing. The important thing is I see him—John Starfire, the Chosen One of the whole damn universe, standing in the doorway of the Imperial Senate, and he's shouting something, and I can even feel it, a wave through the universe itself.

It's over.

I'm sweating and bleeding and every one of my muscles is as wrung and worn as old rope. The sweet planetside air of Irithessa tastes beautiful. Even the smoke tastes beautiful.

I raise my soulsword and cheer, too, as much as I can. The synth-fibers stretch in my reconstructed tongue, the wires in my reconstructed muscle strain, the wounds beneath the surface always evident.

Cheer for freedom and all that crazing shit. Cheer most of all for my friends, the unlucky bastards who didn't live to see today. I'm here, now, cheering in your place.

A thousand exhausted arms raise a thousand bloody soulswords into the smoky air of the City Imperial.

John Starfire takes his soulsword to his own arm, cutting a fine line across the skin. His blood runs down the channels of the sword and catches fire, a bright, white corona that gleams over the crowd, sends ripples of light up the black-and-white banner behind him. He lowers the sword and the crowd starts buzzing.

"Did you get that, sir?" Rashiya asks me, when I turn around. Her face is streaked with carbon, and the strip of circuit in her temple is flickering. The synthskin around it is half melted. Her synthskin is a remnant from the same battle that took my original tongue, a chunk of my leg, and a couple of my original fingers. We are damn lucky these are our only souvenirs.

"No," I slur. "Let me guess. Glorious victory. Go back to the lines."

"Not quite." She smiles, and she can't help herself—she touches my arm, her green eyes alive and shining. Her red hair is slick with sweat, and it makes her look damn good.

Yes, she's my subordinate and we shouldn't have become involved, but even vat-cooked crosses have got to keep warm. Hell, I don't need to explain myself. I'm a goddamn war hero. "Find a place to bunk. Looters will be shot. Food's fair game."

"Shot. Right."

"I need to make sure that Helthizor's all right," she says. "That kid took quite a hit in the leg." She touches my hair. "You need to get some rest. I didn't know you had this in you."

"Had what?" I say.

"You took out two gun posts in less than an hour. Don't you remember?"

"It blurs."

She, in defiance of all sense and regulation, moves close and hugs me, and whispers in my ear, "The dead can finally rest easy."

I can't help it. I put a hand in her hair and hold her close.

"You rest too," she says.

"Not a chance. Stamp your boots and open your sheath," I say.

"Aye, sir."

And then I go, away, away from the crowd full of milling soldiers, away from where the main conflict spilled over from the aerial campaign, past the ancient crystal pyramids and shattered grav-tracks, into the darkened canyons of the city.

That is to say, I go places that any soldier should know better than to go a few hours after battle.

So half an hour after I've won the glorious victory for the Resistance, I find myself kneeling in a dirty alley between two Kurguls, who are holding guns to my head because I tried to steal their drugs.

"You know I'm a war hero, right?" I say.

They don't say a word. Their little tentacled mouths curl up and they rattle their vestigial wings under their ugly carapaces. Just waiting on a command from their local nest queen to wipe me. One mutters a string of grunts. The other says something I actually understand, which means he must want me to hear it. "No one will miss another Jorian cross."

"No one will," I agree. "I don't know why you're waiting on approval. Your nest is most likely dead."

The one on the left pushes his gun into the back of my skull. "Toss the soulsword," the Kurgul says, "and we'll give you a clean death."

Kurguls. Superstitious bastards, the lot of them. They'll shoot a Jorian, but they want us to be far from our weapon.

Soulswords have quite a reputation among the religious. "Despite the name, these things only take your memories, fellas. They're neuron-keyed. If I could take souls, I might have something worth keeping."

I draw the sword. The Kurguls grip their weapons, ready to riddle me with shards if I make a move.

I toss the soulsword down the alley and sink to my knees.

"Do it. Give me some drugs or kill me." Their shard-rifles heat up. I close my eyes, and feel the relief I've been waiting for, for ages. I can see my friends' faces. Not like the last time I saw their faces, when they were just bits of meat torn from the bone and scattered across the hallway. No, my friends are smiling now, still breathing.

The Kurguls scream and shards whistle past my ear with a rush of heat. I open my eyes.

Rashiya is standing there, holding a shard-rifle of her own. The Kurguls are both missing their heads. She is not watching their corpses. She is looking at me, and her eyes are narrowed, reddened.

I stand up. Still not dead. "Stamp your boots and open your sheath," I say, with my best half-cocked smile.

Someone else walks out from behind her. I drop to one knee.

"Get up, Araskar," says John Starfire himself. "My daughter here told me about you. The war's not over."

"You have an Imperial minute to explain yourself," Rashiya says.

"You can't pull rank on me, Lieutenant." I've been waiting

for the day my luck would run out, but I figured it would be a hot shard tearing out my brain, not my one friend and bed-mate turning out to be the daughter—the *daughter!*—of the Chosen One himself. Do you know what I've done with this woman? Does her *father* know?

"You're going to be sleeping outside an airlock tonight unless you explain yourself."

I sit there for a minute, trying to read into her words as much as I can. I don't think she heard me talk about the drugs. Good. "We won," I say. "There wasn't anything left for me."

"I'm not anything," she says.

"Damn it, you know what I mean," I say. And then, because I'm winning the war of idiocy too, I say, "Actually, you don't."

It's the funny thing about being a cross. You never get a real family, unless you're one of those odd cases, like Rashiya, whose parents managed to reproduce. If you're like me, your vat batch is your family. And my batch mates, my battalion, all my best friends, died the moment they boarded our first Impe-rial vessel, turned to blood and meat by shard-fire. Only I, last out of the burrowing pod, survived.

Then I killed half that ship with my own vat-grown hands. Got the Resistance's highest medal for it. Irony's a cold bitch, ai?

"The war's over, Rashiya. Now I've got no reason for them all to be dead and me to be here."

She turns to the door. "That's your answer. That."

Well, that and the fact that I've been doing so many drugs that I ought to get another medal for surviving. "You didn't come from a batch, Rash. You don't know what it's like."

She turns back to me, her face cold as stone. "My father wants a word with you, so I won't kill you now. I saved your burning life today, sir, so I expect that next time I see you you'll be more grateful." She opens the door and leaves me in the cell. I lie back and stare up at the ceiling.

Her pater comes in.

Until a little while ago, I had only seen the guy in our newsreels. In person, he looks older, his hair and beard more white than black. Tall. Strong. Every bit the hero, except he's got his hand on his soulsword hilt, clutching it, releasing and clutching again. I guess when you've spent that much time fighting, that's what happens.

He sits on the bed next to me. Right next to me. He puts his hand, the one not twitching on his hilt, on my leg.

"That took a beating," he says. He rolls up his sleeve—simple black shirt for John Starfire, no Vanguard uniform. His arm is a map of scars, over slashes of steel mesh. "I lost the entire arm at Daruthal," he says. "And most of this leg. My face was still okay. That was a relief to Aranella, my wife."

"I know," I say. Aiya, do I sound stupid. You'd think I could get rid of that slurring voice for the Hero of the Galaxy himself. "I read about it." Come on, Araskar, speak like a man before this guy takes his soulsword to your man-parts.

"What else have you read about?" His eyes twinkle, like a proper old man. "I'm interested."

I try to think. It's tough to think through this relief, given that he hasn't yet told me to fall on my short soulsword. "The news says you took down old Emperor Turka in a proper sword fight."

"I wish. I had the Vanguard put us in a room together, just like he wanted. That blueblood bastard ran, and I couldn't get him to turn and face me, so I gave up and opened him from spine to shitter."

He laughs. I laugh too, because I figure he's trying to put me at ease. That's more frightening than the alternative.

"Araskar, I'm not sure whether to treat you as a disobedient subordinate, or my daughter's suitor."

What's a man supposed to say to that? "Ass is chapped either way, sir."

And then his face turns serious. "Have you read the Third Book?"

That would be the scripture that foretold the coming of John Starfire himself. As I said, my ass is chapped, so I tell the truth. "Didn't have much time for reading in the last few years." I used to like reading. Had the full collection of the Scurv Silvershot comic books, in real paper. They burned up somewhere outside the orbit of Brathaag, where all our supplies for the Larthe'ea campaign vanished. Lost my guitar, too.

"Do you believe the prophecy?"

Another one of those hard questions. "We're here, sir."

He sighs. "We are here. We are here, and I'm still not sure if I believe it. You'd think I would know whether or not I really was the man in the scriptures, but there's a lot of it that didn't happen the way it was prophesied. Am I the son of stars? Are the bluebloods the children of giants?" He draws his soulsword—about time, way he's been clutching it. "Like these. The legends say that a Jorian soulsword was a thing of miracles. Could cut through anything in the universe. Could draw the essence of the Starfire into it, the fuel that burns in pure space. But these are metal with psychic resonators built in, made in a factory and matched to the psychic signature of crosses that come from the vats downstairs. Still, these swords, and those vat-cooked crosses, have won the galaxy back."

I curse myself for saying it, but I have to ask. "What about your sword?"

"Mine?"

"It do what they say?" I nod toward his soulsword. "Like in the legends? It can bring a soul back?"

"No," John Starfire says. "No, I'm afraid that if there are any soulswords like that, they're lost to the ages."

Well, I got my chance to ask that.

He looks at me with those crystal blue eyes. "My people believe I am the Chosen One, and so I have to act that way, and destroy the threats to my people. You"—here he taps my rebuilt leg—"are a hero, and whether you believe so or not, you have to act that way."

"Yes, sir."

He stands up. "The war isn't over, Araskar. It won't be over for a long time. The blueblood stain—that human stain—is everywhere." His hand is back on the soulsword hilt, clutching and pawing it unconsciously. *Human* stain? "There's at least ten thousand crosses still coming out of functioning vats, and the remnants of the Empire control most of them. We have new conscripts, kids who need brave commanders. They have new conscripts, too. Consolidation is going to be long, hard work."

Like I suspected. Glorious victory. Go back to the lines.

"I want you for the Vanguard," he says. That one wakes me up. "My closest circle. You'll be one of five Secondblades under Firstblade Terracor, leading a specially trained division."

"Sir . . . thank you?" I didn't mean it to come out as a question, but . . . "Me? Why the hell me?"

"Rank means many things, Lieutenant. In this case, it means survival."

There it is. He's going to put me in charge of some little half-trained slugs, so that I don't go offing myself.

"I need men like you. And if I catch you chasing trouble with Kurguls, the only Secondblade you'll see will be the one that takes your head off."

I can't help asking. "Rashiya?"

"I've got another mission for her." He pauses. "I didn't help her, Araskar. She joined on her own, and it wasn't until a few days ago that I knew she had survived. Respect that."

"Right."

"Get some sleep," he says. He takes that twitchy hand off his hilt and puts it on my arm. "Stamp your boots and open your sheath." And then his hand goes right back to the hilt.

I stand up and salute as he turns to go. Vanguard. Little slugs like me don't become Vanguard. All I've ever done was kill a bunch of other crosses. Once I got command, I tried to keep my kids together, but we lost plenty of them. I could have been shot down in Irithessa's orbit, in planetfall, in the assault on the capital. I'm only here by luck. And as for respecting Rashiya, I was. She deserves someone a lot better.

I sink back down, and dig around in my pocket. I pull out a handful of the little pink pills that were so much trouble to get from those Kurguls.

They sit in the hollow of my hand, five dots.

The Kurguls call these brain bullets. Most folk just call them pinks. They're simple tranquilizers as far as the galaxy is concerned. Unless you're a Jorian cross.

For one like me, these tranquilizers put you in touch with the beating heart of the universe. It's like music. You have no idea what music can sound like, until you've heard the background music of the stars. Only a few crosses can hear it. I am one of the lucky few, when I take these.

A soft, low whistle like wind through tall trees. Over it, the dropping notes, like cool pinpricks of rain. And when I have these, I don't care about my soldiers. I don't care about Rashiya and all my friends dying on that ship, the Vanguard, the bloody mission.

Winning a war isn't the best feeling of my life. It's up there, but it can't compare to forgetting the war completely.

3

Jaqi

YOU'D BE AMAZED how quick a batch of scabs can clear out a fighting pit. There's not a lot of places to go on an ecosphere only a few miles around, and there are a lot of people crowded in port at Swiney Niney. But everyone from that fighting pit scatters, leaving me alone.

And it just so happens that this fighting pit is deep in what was originally the parkland of Swiney. Probably a nice place, once upon a time, but since the environmental controls broke, this green is now a thick, stinking jungle.

There's pathways here, through mud and roots and all sorts of weird-looking plants. Might lead to another fighting pit, and maybe another sleaze who tosses me in a cage with centipedes—aiya!—and there's plenty of footprints on the paths, but I don't see anyone as I wander over roots and rocks, through mud, and try to ignore the pain in my face and shoulder where the Necro-Thing threw me to the ground.

I wade through mud, keeping one eyeball on the sticky flowers all around me. Probably some carnivorous crossbreed, illegal as living forever, dropped here. They cluster and sprout and get big and toothy on the remnants of those fighting pits. Yep, that's what an ecosphere is like on the edge of wild space. Fun, ai?

The path winds around a small hill, or a giant pile of moss, depending on your point of view. From around the side of the hill, I can see down, back to the port. Concrete buildings huddle against the honeycomb of black tunnels in the air that will take you out of the ecosphere. I was being dragged by the big Rorgs before, so I can't say I paid much attention to the details.

That's when I see a familiar face, frozen on the path ahead of me. Big head, like a melon, all covered with boils, and an eye patch. "Ai! Palthaz? Palthaz Perron!"

He stares in my direction for a minute—Zu-Path, as a race, aren't famous for their wits—and then steps off the path, running up that small hill.

"Wait, Palthaz! It's Jaqi! From Bill's!" I saw this sleaze come in and out of port a thousand times. He's even fatter than he used to be, which means I catch up with him.

"Palthaz!"

He hustles onward. "Not now, Jaqi."

"You remember me! Listen, Palthaz, I'm in an evil way. Between jobs, and I just want something to eat—"

"Run off!" he snarls at me. But of course, I'm still able to keep up with him. He sinks farther into the mud than I do. That's my benefit of never eating.

"Trade you this," I say, and hold up Cade's gun. "Nice piece. Vintage Zarronen A-5. Better than that Keil piece of crap you're carrying."

He eyeballs it. There's no greed like a smuggler's greed. "I— No! Off, Jaqi."

"I will not!" I say. I raise the gun, and he freezes, without a blink. "Give me some damn food!" I'm in pain and hungrier than ever and in no mood for this.

He just sighs, looking down the barrel. "You a cross," he

says. "You're good for food anywhere. Haven't you heard? You rule the galaxy now."

"That don't help me on Swiney Niney," I say.

"I can get some meat for you, but you swear to get away. I can't afford trouble with a cross."

"What kind of meat?"

"Matters, does it?"

"Not really," I say, and lower the gun. "As long as it was breathing once and it's salted now."

He scuttles off.

This is the business of being a smuggler—you're always going to pretend to be a cold bastard. And something has Palthaz spooked evil, enough that he isn't acting like a smuggler should act at all.

So I follow him.

What? This scab is obviously protecting one evil catch. The crickets give good work, but if I can go into mid-galaxy without fear of being conscripted, then Palthaz is a better bet.

Palthaz has done a few legitimate jobs carrying Imperial matter. And apparently being a cross is now a ticket to respectable. I still can't get that through my head. I could go mid-galaxy, if I wanted to.

All the way to Irithessa? Why not? See the capital of the Empire. Will we even call it the Empire anymore? I could wander around them museums, with the remnants of the old galaxy. I could see me a couple of plays, like a lady. I could drink as much as I want and have some real nice times with fancy boys and girls.

Palthaz scuttles into a little tunnel that runs under the hill of green moss. On second look, it en't really a hill. More like a clump of roots, from some tree that's long been cut down. I en't dumb enough to go into the tunnel after him, but if I eyeball the thing right, there's a gap between roots.

I crawl in, scraping my back, squeezing through a thick layer of soil and between two monstrous roots. I squirm on past a big root, and then another, until I see light coming from below. The roots interlock here; a set of rafters for some kind of hidey-hole. Seems like it would be a great spot for a smuggler, but a few things are off—the place is wet, brown water dripping from above (and soaking me, as if I didn't have enough sweat doing so already), and it stinks like that Necro-Thing's armpit. Any smuggler who cared about his goods would have dehumidified the place and cleared it out a bit. This is more of an animal's burrow. This far underground, Palthaz shouldn't have to worry about lighting the place up bright, either. But he doesn't have good light, just a few glowing lamps.

"I need some of the food," Palthaz says. "Bargaining."

Another voice—young man, by the sound of it—says, polite as you please, "I'm sorry, but we need as much food as we can take."

"You'll do fine on protein packs. Learn your place, boy—you en't a damn blueblood no more." That near-panicked note in Palthaz's voice is now blending into anger.

Another voice. Young girl. I squirm around for a look, get lower in the roots until I can see. There are three humans down there with Palthaz. Tall guy, probably about sixteen, on Imperial reckoning. Girl, younger, maybe ten, and little boy, maybe five. They are dirtier than even I am, and haggard, but the clothes they wear are easily real cotton. Before they crawled into this hole, those clothes were evil expensive. Bluebloods on the run.

"I've got a cross on my tail, Quinn!" Palthaz spits the words out.

The teenage boy draws back. "What?"

"If I didn't owe your papa my freedom . . . this en't worth those damn crosses!"

Did Palthaz wrong the Resistance or something? He's muttering now, and I can't hear it. The Resistance couldn't afford to make enemies of smugglers, last I checked.

"We're safe, though," the young girl says. "Right? The machine is still masking us?"

"Long as it works."

So, this is the moment my luck for the day decides to keep on going the way it's been going. I shift around in those roots to get a good look, but the problem with those kind of roots, in swampy ground, is that they shift with you. Like now, when they shift me right out into Palthaz's secret chamber.

Palthaz does fire this time. Good thing he's spooked; he missed even at point-blank. I jump up and shove Cade's gun in his face. "Not a move or you get two eye patches!"

Another barrel rams my back, between my ribs. The teenage boy says, "Don't move, cross, or I'll kill you like you deserve."

4

Araskar

THE MOONS OF KEIL are all fume and furnace; artificially imposed atmosphere, just enough to keep running a weapons manufacturing plant that makes the Dark Zone seem friendly. The air is reverse-cell oxygen that tastes like metal; the fine mist of mud and blood, added to the smoke, almost improves it.

From our muddy pit, the munitions plant looms on the horizon, taking up the sky, stacks and towers upon stacks and towers. Up above a gas-waste ship took a hit and the air itself is still burning, streaks of fire catching in the sky. It's exactly the kind of thing I hoped to be done with by now. Nope, still in the shit. Only now it's not for the glory of the Resistance, it's for the glory of consolidation.

Doesn't have the same ring, does it?

"Sir!" Helthizor, fellow veteran of Irithessa and my new second in command, runs back down the hill, zigzagging, clutching his rifle in a ragged arm. "Must be an entire batch of Marines up there. Stripped of their badges, but definitely Marine-quality crosses."

"A whole batch." I look around at my boys and girls. Squad of fifty, now down by ten. One terrifying planetfall, two days of hard hiking through slaglands, where anything but a vat-grown cross would be poisoned, and here we are, well and truly in hell. "We have the advantage in brains." No one comes out the vats dumber—and tougher—than an Imperial Marine cross. I hold up my comm. "Hold, Helthizor. They don't see us yet."

Helthizor collapses next to me, in the mud. "I don't see how we can finish this mission."

"Keep your mouth shut if that's what comes out," I say. I look around the squad, my little slugs, my reasons for living. Joskiya meets my eyes. Just last week, she passed her translator test. Was in for a promotion, and well deserved, to intelligence, but she passed it up in order to go into this hell with us. I look around and I see a good thirty kids who could have lived long lives elsewhere but took the chance on the Vanguard. I see ten others who have lived through way too much to die here.

All in the name of consolidation.

I grab my comm and signal Terracor, the high-and-mighty Firstblade, head of the Vanguard, and the biggest shit in space. Might be intercepted, so I'm bouncing the wave off a couple of our different signal points, and it takes a minute to register. "Blindside, this is Darkside, you copy?"

A minute later. "Speak clearly, Darkside."

I try to make that fake tongue enunciate. "We got an entire batch of Marines with the suborbital guns. I need support, and I need it now."

"Not until you make a pickup zone." I can practically hear Terracor shaking his head, and it's only the delay in the communiqué that keeps him from interrupting me like always. "They're running targeted EMPs, flame-sheets, and nuke-busters, and they can run them as long as that factory's working."

There's only one answer to that. "Understood. I guess

we'd better shut down the factory."

"No one will judge if you pull back," he says. "I called for a planet-cracker."

"There's a hell of a lot of innocent folk on this moon," I say. "I won't crack it."

"Mostly humans," Terracor says. "We don't *need* the moon."

I shut the comm off. Terracor's useless once he gets on the subject of humans. Seems like all my superiors are. I get that the bluebloods were all humans, but not all humans are bluebloods.

I look back at Helthizor. "Any chance you caught the make of their big guns?"

Ten minutes later, I'm telling all of them the orders, watching their faces as they all realize that this is probably it, the mission that ends them.

Irony continues her legendary career as a cold bitch. Being vat-cooked crosses, my freshly trained slugs look, for the most part, exactly like my dead friends. Helthizor has the same template as my batch-mate Barathuin, that same heavy set of shoulders, young-looking face, and for all that he's not the swordsman Barathuin was, they even hold their blades the same. I was with Barathuin when we picked our *names*. We lost our virginity the same night. He's gone, and here's his replacement, about to get killed again. Joskiya looks just like Karalla, she who carried around that projectile weapon for years and never got to use it.

Almost makes you think the Empire had it right, the way they don't give their crosses names.

My hands are shaking. I close my eyes and think of the little pink pills. *Just keep these slugs alive, and you can go back to the music.*

"Helthizor, you wait for the signal, and then you bug on up

the hill too. No tougher than crawling up the Bastard," I tell them, referring to the hill we trained on back on Irithessa. "Be glad I made you do extra sessions. Stamp your boots and open your sheath."

They repeat it. "Stamp your boots and open your sheath."

I really don't think this will work.

We zig and zag up the muddy hill, until I can see the emplacement just above us. Three big guns, shipbreakers, meant for suborbital heavy fire. As Helthizor said, they're Keil standard make. Oh, and there's also every other kind of gun you could imagine—gatling, rifles, rockets, good old pistols, and each Marine wears a scarred soulsword. The mud gleams red, reflecting the shards in the guns that are heating up.

I signal Salleka. She's covered herself in mud, and squirms through the red-lit ground slowly, toward the first of the big guns. By some miracle, the Marines don't spot her, so she just has to squirm through a little wire—those EMPs make it so a shard-field won't stay up, so the Marines are only guarded by old-fashioned thin wires.

I sit there and hold my breath. I would go myself, if there weren't so many rules about the Secondblade doing things like that. Still feels wrong to let these kids take all the risks.

Time for Joskiya. She's even muckier than Salleka, and she squirms along, real close to the ground, just like a worm in the mud—but one of those Marines spots her and opens up. He gets her right in the head. The shard flashes bright red, takes a divot out of the mud, tosses her brain-bits everywhere.

Kid should have taken that promotion.

The Marines are searching for us now. I signal Salleka—she's alone out there now—and I hiss, "Fire!" into the comm. From below, Helthizor sends a jet of fire arcing across the sky; from the Marines' perspective, it could be a low-level flare-up from the gas-waste ship, or an attack. They fire over us, at his position, and Salleka scrambles under the heavy gun; working quick, she breaks open the panel underneath.

Keil guns, even the big shipbreakers, are cheap. Only takes a few crossed wires to blow one up.

My third, Iniyor, crawls through the mud toward the second gun, past Joskiya's body, but another Marine has his eyes open, and he sees her and hits her, leaves her wounded, moaning in the mud—maybe dying, maybe alive—if we don't make some gains, the med bots won't be able to figure it out.

They change the direction of their fire, too close to our location, kicking mud up into my eyes. But Salleka's finished with the first big gun; she slips away into the mud, over the barrier and toward the second gun. She gets tangled up going back through that wire. Not moving fast enough.

The big guns all have to go, or this moon gets cracked, and us with it. So I stand up.

They turn their fire, and I run, and the only thing I have to knock those shards aside is my damn *soulsword,* but my little slugs stand up and cover me, firing enough that they take out a good chunk of the Marines. I slide in under the second big suborbital gun just as the first one goes.

Salleka did good work. The first big gun blows all its artillery-grade shards and takes all the Marines around it to pieces. I get the second one wired well enough before a shard blasts away a good chunk of the synthskin on my bad leg. I stand up and it's close quarters; I immediately lock a soulsword with some Marine who has a death wish. I push him hilt-to-hilt and then I turn him around, shove him against the gun just as it blows.

Artillery-grade shards break apart from the big gun, hit the Marine, rip apart his armor, rip apart his skin. He shields me fair well. I go flying, holding the soggy meat that was the Marine's body, and I land in a mess of weaponry, my ears ringing, my skin burning. The third big gun has toppled over. I lash out with my soulsword, grab my pistol. Can't see much, or hear a thing. I'm just striking at nearby shapes until one of my squad gets behind me and pulls me down the hill.

"Stay down, sir," says the fuzzy voice of one of my slugs.

"Hell no." Through my blurry vision, this slug looks like Rashiya. No, can't be Rashiya. Rashiya had a unique face, home-grown.

"Sir?"

"I'm not dead yet!" I stand up and shove my body forward.

It's all grit-work from there. Enough Marines are left that we have to try and cut them off from the weapons depot, and there's plenty of sword-to-sword, plenty of shards in the head, but my little slugs are tougher even than these tough bastards.

One Marine gets away, goes up the hill toward their bunker. I chase him, for all that my vision is still blurring and the metal bones of my leg are exposed. I chase him right into the dark bunker. Stupid. Once I get in there, he's holding a charge and it's flashing red, lighting up his face.

He's older. Mess of scars and wrinkles. First time I've seen an Imperial cross who lived more than a few months.

He doesn't throw the charge. "Why?" he asks.

I raise my pistol.

He talks again. "Your leader has sold us out to the devil, boy. All to get rid of a few humans."

I keep my pistol trained on the guy. If he throws that charge, we're both dead. If I shoot him, I might get out in time. But . . . "You got information, you can come in."

He laughs and shakes his head. "I've been to the Dark Zone. I've looked the devil in the face. Your John Starfire is no different. You watch, boy. It's not going to end at bluebloods, or even at humans, not till the whole galaxy goes dark."

He presses the activator and throws the charge.

I catch it and throw it back.

I toss myself backward in time for the bunker to blow, and roll down the hill, fetching up against some nice sharp rocks.

Not dead yet.

We've almost made the place presentable a day later, when Firstblade High-and-Mighty Terracor comes to see me. We've got pets—local scavengers, equal parts black feathers and thin scaly tail, tearing into the flesh still left after we burned the bodies. That's the kind of life that finds a foothold on a weapons-making moon. We've got bunks—in the mud away from the depot, given that we're still sitting on a mountain full of shards, and of course, the latrines are properly stinking. You'd think, with all the work that folk do in the vats, someone could make a cross that didn't have to shit. It's as close to a home as I ever get.

Terracor's face is its usual scowl above the black beard. He sits down across from me, and doesn't even take the rations bar I offer. It's a good thing I just came down from a good five-hour session with the music. I can about stand his cold-ass face.

"Scored you a weapons deposit," I say. "You could say thank you."

"I'm not going to thank you for taking this kind of risk," he says.

"The Vanguard always takes point," I say. It's how they got their reputation. Terracor wants me to pull back a bit, manage the missions from the ship's deck, but I'm not about to do that—I would have to take double the drugs I am already taking to live with myself.

Terracor sits next to me. "I'm worried about the human," he says. "The owner of these weapons."

"Someone I should know about?"

"Formoz of Keil. Head of Keil Quality Vats."

"I know that name," I say. "That's the fella who diverted my whole batch to the Resistance. Sent a good number of the crosses from his vats to freedom. I ought to shake his hand." It takes a minute to register. "You telling me that this—all this—was owned by a *sympathizer*?"

"He's dead," Terracor says. "You can't shake his hand."

"Wait, why the hell did we attack a facility that was owned by a sympathizer? Why were there Imperial Marines protecting it?" He doesn't answer. "I asked you an important question, sir. I have a right to—"

"I'm not convinced I can trust you, Araskar."

Funny thing: Terracor comes from my same template. Only his thicker beard and a scar on his forehead mark him apart. But I've never had any of my slugs mistake us, because I could never look that much of a cold bastard, calling in a planet-cracker for one weapons depot.

"I suspect, sir"—I only call him that when I want to grate his skin—"that you are under orders to tell me the truth about this mission." And if he won't, the Resistance be damned, I'm taking my slugs and going home.

He stares at me. One of his eyes is synth, vat-grown replacement nerves; you couldn't tell. "Formoz of Keil, who owned this facility, had high-level intel. My orders were to secure the moon by whatever measures the Vanguard could take." He sighs. "But, apparently, Formoz bugged out in an escape ship, right when the battle began, and was shot down by some random gunner. So he had some kind of intel, leaked from levels even above me, and now we have no idea."

These pieces are not coming together. "Terracor, this Formoz was a supporter of the Resistance. And you're telling me that we attacked his own facility, charged in, and— Dark take me, did he actually hire Imperial Marines to *protect* him from the Resistance?"

"You need to stop asking so many questions, Secondblade."

I'm too angry to shut up. "Tell me there was a good reason for today, or I walk."

"Sympathizer or no, the owner was one of them," Terracor says.

"Bluebloods?"

"Humans."

I can't think what to say to that. Who cares whether a mark is human?

"The next mission is going to be a nice break for you, Araskar. I'm taking fifty of your division, you, and me after Formoz's children. Three kids, on the run. Word has it that they are connected to the intel. Should be a simple snatch-and-grab."

I stand up. "Why do you care about children? Who would pass along high-level intel to children? This all stinks, stinks worse than I do right now."

Terracor stands up, too, faces me. Sadly, given the leg replacement, I am now unnaturally shorter than my template here, so I have to glare up. "You won't ask any more questions about this mission, Secondblade." He turns to walk out the door, and pauses, to look back at me. The smoky light catches his vat-grown eye, turns it white. "Araskar."

"Yes."

"Ever heard the expression 'nits will make lice'?"

"No."

He gives a little half laugh, and walks out. I sit back down.

Did my slugs die today for the sake of intel, or just for the sake of some crazing crusade against humans? It can't be. It can't be that the Resistance, after all this time, after all we fought for, is wasting us. Not after I won a war for the Resistance. Not after my friends, and my little slugs, died.

It can't be.

I hardly realize I have the handful of pills out, until they're in my mouth. I know I just came down, but sometimes there's only one place to go.

5

Jaqi

GUNS TO MY BACK, Necro-Things. No tomatoes. This is a day. "All right," I say. "I'm going to turn around, evil slow."

"Do not move," the boy says.

Palthaz snorts. "Quinn, don't waste a shard on this one. Jaqi, what in the Dark are you doing?"

"Thought you were protecting a big score," I say. No point in hiding it. Palthaz gives some long rumble that is probably his people's moan of despair. Or he's got gas.

The barrel unsticks itself from my ribs and I turn around. I get a good look at this Quinn. Handsome kid, though he shows some signs of being soft. Got some serious bags under his eyes for seventeen. He's muddy and hasn't seen a shower in longer than I have (long, aiya, much too long, in case you need to know). He's shaking. Nervous, and en't handling life without food or sleep well.

The girl and the little boy behind him huddle together. They too en't slept proper, by the look of them. I'm used to that, but that's how they make crosses, built to take a lot of punishment. Normal humans can't take more than a few days without shutting their eyes.

I eyeball the gun he's still holding on me, his hand shaking on the handle and trigger. More Keil quickies; probably cost him twenty at most. "Here." I hold up Cade's shotgun, by the barrel. "I'll give you this for some real matter. Produce. Coffee?" Not a move. "Come on now, you'll get more life, and more shots out of that. It isn't some quick-cranked synth steel heap." I hold up the extra shard-charges I took off Cade's body. "This beauty is all analog. Just levers and locks. For a piece of bacon?"

Not a word to me, not a word to Palthaz; he just clutches that crap gun. I'm starting to think this kid will really shoot. Well, once he realizes he left the safety on.

"Hell of a deal."

"You're a cross," he says. "We can't trust a word you say."

"Quinn," Palthaz says. "This one en't smart enough to join the Resistance."

"Walk out the airlock, Palthaz," I say.

"You en't," Palthaz said. "Galaxy's full of truth, don't make any sense to ignore it. You want to make catch, Jaqi? Stay here and keep that antique primed. I need a point man. I was out trying to find my burning contact when you stumbled in." He looks at Quinn. "She's harmless. Don't know a thing about the Resistance. And she'll do anything for coin or food."

"Thanks for the recommendation," I say.

"Say a word, leave your post, steal any food, and you go right out Swiney's airlock," Palthaz says. He fingers that eye patch and heads out.

Quinn's staring after Palthaz like he's just lost his puppy.

"You bluebloods?" I ask Quinn. "Ai, Quinn? You can put the gun down."

He looks at his gun, back at me. "You're a cross."

"Yes. Nice of you to notice. You ever fired that gun?"

"No," the little girl says from behind him.

"Kalia!"

"It's true," she says. "It's not a lie. I think she's okay, Quinn. If Palthaz trusts her, we should."

"Trust" is a strong word for how Palthaz feels about me, but I smile for the kid. "Kalia, you're called?"

"This is Toq." She points to the five-year-old who is nestled in her arms, his eyes never leaving me. "I'm Kalia. We're from Keil. Our dad owns Keil Quality Vats."

"We aren't bluebloods," Quinn says. "We were helping the Resistance."

"But my dad said that the Vanguard was coming, and we were better off-planet," she said. "I don't know why. He helped the Vanguard. He sent off all those crosses last year. They were the ones that go all rebellious. Aberrations." She's practiced that word.

"It's more complicated than that, Kalia," Quinn says.

"I know," she says, emphasizing the words, "but since you won't tell me *anything,* I have to only say what I know." She glares shard-fire at him.

"So," I say. "Your pater was on the right side of the Resistance, and now they've got the galaxy by the balls, he's suddenly on the wrong side?"

Quinn looks at his brother and sister. "We had an agreement with the Resistance. They broke the agreement, and then Dad said we had to get out."

"Out of mid-galaxy? Is that why you're on the edge of wild space?"

"Out of known space," Quinn said. "He said there wasn't any hope for us here. In the entire galaxy."

I whistle. "You're not going to have much luck in the wild worlds. Unless you're planning to go to the Dark Zone."

"No!" the little boy says.

"He's afraid of the Dark Zone," the girl says. "We had a nanny who used to tell us stories about it."

"Good sense, to be afraid of the devil," I say.

"Dad fired her," Quinn says, ignoring me. He laughs, that kind of bitter angry laugh when the universe's riddles have just become obvious. "Of course, what did it matter? It's not the Dark Zone we're in trouble from, it's the Resistance."

"Did you say you're hungry, Jaqi?" Kalia says. "We have bread and sausage. I can make you a sandwich."

Now there is something to be made of this day. "You're the sweetest thing since strawberries," I say. "I can't remember the last time someone made me a sandwich."

"No more food, Kalia," Quinn says. "We've already eaten half of it."

"Toq is hungry, too, so we might as well make sandwiches for everyone," Kalia says, and points at me. "She looks like she hasn't eaten in a week." That's about right. "Where are you from, Jaqi?"

Nice gets you in a lot of trouble in the wild worlds, but not where she's from. Sure sign of money—they had a real catch back home, I bet. "I'm from all over," I say. Can't decide whether to be my usual cagey or honest, given the circumstances. "I en't vat-grown. My folks were. They escaped and became farmworkers."

"Oh," Kalia says. "You like, picked crops?"

"Right," I said. "Good stuff, sometimes, like tomatoes and strawberries. Other times we just packed corn and seed germ of every kind imaginable. The stuff the big places turn into protein packs."

"I know," Kalia said. "Dad owned a protein plant for a while.

He took us there." She looks to be pondering for something important to say on the subject of a protein plant. She settles for, "It smelled funny."

"I want a sandwich," the five-year-old, Toq, says. "And I want you to read me a story."

"Where is Palthaz?" Quinn says. "How big is this ecosphere? How hard can it be to find who he's looking for?" He's trying, by those squirms, to keep from glaring at me. "I read the entry for this place. It's tiny, as ecospheres go. I thought everyone would know each other."

"Whole galaxy's in a fuss," I say. "Might be you could tell me more about it?"

"You haven't read the news?" Kalia asks.

"I've been out in the wild," I say. "Tell me." Sure would be nice not to have to do this. Why does every filthy scab in the galaxy know how to read except me?

"The Resistance took Irithessa a month ago," Quinn says.

"And the Empire didn't burn them to bits?"

"They seized control of the Imperial nodes," Quinn says. I nod along. You can't travel faster than light without a working node, established by the old Jorians who knew how to make doors into pure space and wire them up to node-engines, to jump other ships.

There's supposed to be no way to travel the galaxy without the Imperial nodes. Of course, nodes have been reordered and discarded a billion times over in the long history of the Empire, and there's plenty of those doors that should be shut, but they got hacked and maintained by the sorts who hang out in places like Swiney Niney. In the deep black, a pirate node means business, a private route. And you can either get a Suit, one of the mechanical men, to hack it for you, and give you the codes to open it, or you can find a cross who can move you in and out of pure space by finding the nodes herself.

That's me.

"So what'd the Resistance do once they got the network?"

"John Starfire shut the military nodes," Quinn says, "and left the Navy in the Dark Zone. Only a couple of ships escaped. A hundred million Marines were left there." He clears his throat. "Without resupply, the Shir in the Dark Zone will eat them alive."

"Shh," I hiss, afore he even finishes. "I got enough bad luck, Quinn, I don't need you naming the devil."

He turns and fixes me with a look somewhere between a glare and some kind of hope. "You're a criminal, aren't you?"

I hold my hands up. "I have to eat."

"I'm sure you don't do anything evil," Kalia says.

The pay was evil big. "Running guns. Got them through a pirate and sold them through Kurgul nests. The Resistance was a big customer, truth."

They don't know what to say to that.

Kalia hands me a sandwich. The kids complain that the bread is soggy and the meat—more of that slimy thing—tastes funny and I have no idea what they mean, because as I chomp it down, I figure this sandwich is about the greatest thing in the whole galaxy and I would have joined the Resistance for this sandwich, woulda stabbed Emperor Turka my own self for this thing made of real grain grown in real ground and real animals eating real grass.

Once I finish the sandwich, which happens much too quick, I have to admit that perhaps Palthaz has been distracted. Going by Cade, there's a whole lot of sleazy business going down here on Swiney Niney, and the fallout from the Empire's, um, fallout is going to make it worse.

Quinn, as if he's guessed what we're thinking, says, "Palthaz will be back. We have an agreement."

This fella. "I hate to tell you, but Palthaz makes a good living ripping folk off."

"He's bound to keep it," Quinn says, half as if to convince himself. "He's got to."

I'm guessing, by the delay, that Palthaz's contact en't shown, and en't going to show. The well thing to do would be to take the kids back to his ship, keep them hidden till he can reroute.

I don't trust Palthaz to do the well thing.

I also reckon that whoever popped Cade's brainpan is roaming around, looking for these kids. This is good hiding, but it won't last. Next scheduled rain will drown them, for one.

"Might be he keeps his promises," I say, "but there en't no reason to sit here rotting in this hole much longer, waiting for destiny. You're better off waiting back on his ship." I crawl out of the main tunnel and look down the path. Not much to see but the green of Niney, stretching down to the empty square.

"Come on out," I say. "I can take you to Palthaz's ship. You can wait for him there. I reckon the port authority en't paying much attention, on a day like today."

They don't fight me. It occurs to me that they might not be worth the trouble, but I like these little humans. Can't help but like someone who gives you that food. Suppose I'll take one more big risk before I head off into normal life.

Kalia is carrying a funny black square, no visible circuits or buttons. "That your scrambler?" I ask.

"As long as we carry it, no Jorian should be able to sense us," she says.

"Not from afar," I say. "You get close enough to a cross,

those things en't worth a shit in space." That might be a bit rough for these fancies. "I mean . . ."

Kalia giggles. "I never heard that before. A shit in space!"

Quinn's face is blanched. "They can sense you, even with a scrambler field?"

"Never heard of a field that could mask you if a cross comes aside." Still, the kids are protected as long as we stay away from crosses . . .

So we sneak down the path. I get a good look at the packs they're carrying. More real food? Lots of the bulging, familiar squares of protein packs. I ought to throw my lot in with some chefs one of these days.

We sneak around the edges of the market, by the stone moss-and-ivy-eaten buildings that hold goods. En't much to be seen, but I swear I hear scabs talking. "Palthaz's ship is in port Q-36," Quinn says.

"It'll take a minute to get through the port tunnels and find one ship," I say. I eyeball the black honeycomb of tunnels, dotting the fake sky of Swiney's walls. Easy enough to get out of here, I think.

"Jaqi, look . . ." Quinn says.

I turn around and who is there but Zaragathora, Eater of Flesh, all seven feet and tattoos of him. "Where's the money?" His hand lashes out, catches me by the neck. "What do you have?"

6

Jaqi

IT'S HARD TO SAY anything when a big Zarra is clutching your throat and lifting you off the ground, you know? I wish he would have thought about that, because he keeps yelling "Money!" like he expects me to respond.

Quinn shoves his piece into Z's back. The Zarra seems entirely unconcerned by this business. "Money!"

"She doesn't have any money!" the girl, Kalia, yells. "Please!"

He twists his head, which gives me time to kick him good beneath the ribs. He doesn't let go, but I get my fingers inside his grip, pull it away from my neck, enough to croak out, "En't no money!"

He snarls and tosses me. Good toss, that. I fly halfway across the square and bounce along on my tailbone, rattling my teeth. Then I come to rest on a sharp rock, right in my ribs.

I look up and see a lady watching me. She's got her face wrapped up in gray cloth, hiding her mouth. A couple of springs of red hair escape that cloth. Her green eyes are locked on mine, and she's got her hand inside her cloak, massaging some kind of piece. And she's making my brain buzz even harder than the pain from Z's mighty toss.

A Jorian cross.

If I had any doubt, she yanks out a soulsword, right there. The black blade sucks in the light, at least until she slashes her hand like she's cutting bread, and the blood jumps up the blade, springing a white kind of flame. She must be the one killed Cade.

I get up and fall down again. "Aiya, nice sword, now go run off—"

And Quinn, his mind gone to space, runs out into the square—to protect me? To protect his brother and sister? Can't say, but he yells, "Leave her alone! It's not her you want!"

Oh, Dark Stars. "No," I say, sounding space-gone myself, "it is definitely me you want, uh, ignore him . . ." I get up. Then I fall down, because my legs just give out.

This gray-clad Jorian has whirled on Quinn. He's standing there staring at her.

He raises his piece-of-shit Keil gun and fires. She catches the shards on her soulsword, splits them, sends them flying overhead, spinning through the air like feathers. He tries to fire again, but the gun jams.

Can't even think such a thing—a sixteen-year-old kid, a rich kid with not a moment in his life to compare to this shithole at the end of space, never a time he's been in this kind of danger, staring down his own death, realizing it's his own death, realizing he can't do anything about it. His face goes all pale, and sweat pours down his forehead and a couple of damn tears run down his face. His mouth opens like he's trying to say something.

I jump to my feet—finally—and run. "Get out, Quinn!" I don't know what I'm thinking. I en't thinking I can take a trained Jorian with her soulsword primed, but maybe I can yank Quinn away.

I en't gone five steps before she runs Quinn through.

I scream—something—might be a curse, might be crying. I leap at that cross, while she still has her blade in Quinn, sucking his memories. I carry her to the ground, scratching and biting and every dirty blow I ever learned in the spaceways. My tackle pulls her soulsword out of Quinn's body.

I scramble up, and she's readying that soulsword, but I drive a good knuckle-cracker right into her teeth, knock her on her ass.

I grab Quinn's body and scramble backward, and for the first time this day, my luck turns well, because a dozen voices shout in the Kurgul tongue, and shard-fire starts flying thicker than the mosquitoes, and this gray woman cross has to duck and cover.

Quinn's mind is only half gone, that soulsword not having been in his meat long enough to take the memories. But it did plenty of damage. Blood bubbles up Quinn's throat. He tries to speak as I drag him away from the fight. He's in a real bad place, and he's whispering a name—his sister's. He looks at me, and I realize he's trying to ask me something, then he's dead.

Damn kid. Damn me, for taking them out of that hole.

Shards fly everywhere. In a place like Swiney, where just about everyone is doing a scabby deal, one death trips every trigger finger. I hate it, but I have to drop Quinn's dead body.

Me and the kids run from the firefight. En't never run like this, trying to make every stride longer. Z runs right next to me, loping strides eating up the soupy ground, and then he's staring back at me, because he's pulled ahead. "Run!" he says—well, it's more like a roar—"You soft meat, run!"

Toq, the boy, stumbles and falls, and his sister, holding his hand, goes down with me. Kid just saw his brother die, and not even a soul gone free, but half sucked up into some crazy cross's soulsword. And Kalia is crying. And the ship en't getting any closer. And I've got just a few charges left in Cade's gun.

And—gray-clothes is chasing us.

I grab the kids, hoist them to their feet. Z swings Toq up onto his shoulders like a sack, and we run.

In a place as shady as Swiney Niney, there's a couple thousand ways in and out of the port. Folks build enough private tunnels, side tunnels, hidden trapdoors, and eventually the custom officers don't try to keep up—they just blow you out of the sky if you en't paid the proper bribes, and let you get to port the way you want. So we see a mighty honeycomb of tunnels come up, and it's both good and bad news.

"Kalia, I need you to think. Think. Which one did you come—"

"You stupid meat!" Z snatches the gun out of my hand. "No time!" He fires a dozen shards off at the cross.

Gray-clothes raises her soulsword and the shards split, fly away, break into flickers of light. Damn. That is one juiced cross.

"Give me that." I snatch the gun away from Z. "Kalia, Toq, get in the tunnels!"

"Are you—" Z cuts himself off. "If you have magic, do it."

Ha.

I shoot again.

Again she throws the shards off like they're nothing. Damn, damn damn.

I'm a cross. In theory, I have the same powers she has. Right?

But I can't do else, so I reach out like I reach out for nodes, same way I reach out when I'm going into faster-than-light space. Feel around for a node, except this time—

I feel it. Like she's screaming in my head.

I push at her like I push when I open a node—and damn, I don't know if it's doing a thing, but I squeeze that trigger.

She raises her hand, but the shards don't splinter. They batter her backward, blast her face and chest. She en't bleeding, but she's thrown against the nearest wall by the force of the shot.

Well, Starfire bless me and shit my pants. I did something . . . Jorian.

Z lets off that good, long roar, and starts for her prone body. I grab Z's arm—a bit like grabbing a clump of molded steel—and pull. "Come on! Come on!" I could use this slab.

"I'm not leaving this undone."

"They'll kill you! Come on, the money! Those kids are worth money!"

He tosses me into the tunnels. The gravity-wells suck me up, spin me around, and down I go.

The tunnel spits us out into a suspended port hallway, one of the metal arms that extends from the ecosphere. All along the tunnel, periodic openings show the port arms of space-ships and, more often, empty space behind a sense-field as the ships have gone flying off.

The port tunnels are filled with every Swiney Niney scab running for deep space, bouncing along in zero. The lights along the roof are flickering on and off. Roars and vacuum-pops echo as ships tear away, hardly even taking the time to disconnect, breaking bits of plasticene from the port arms, littering space with debris. Kurguls and Rorgs and crickets and Zu-Path are zooming through the stinking zero air, bounding from wall to wall around us.

Right in the middle of this horror show, Kalia and Toq float, holding each other, crying.

Kalia looks up. "Jaqi—I'm sorry—the ship isn't there. It's not here."

Z comes flying out of the tunnel after me and crashes into me, throwing me against the bulkhead, rebounding against him—as if he en't nearly killed me enough today! "Q-36, your brother said. We are . . ." I check the listing on the wall. "Three levels up."

Z grabs the edge of the window and presses his face against it. "What are we looking for?"

Palthaz's ship is a . . . "Zerrek T-15, as I recall?"

"There's one down three levels." He looks at me, those tattoos wrinkling all the wrong ways, because he actually looks, for a second, a bit scared. Before he gets back to snarling. "If no Vanguard. Can you get in?"

Kalia swims up to us, brave girl, looks out the window. "There's a bad lock on one of the hatches. We can break into the ship. But you'd have to get a suit and crawl out along—"

"Later. Let's run."

It's not as hard as you'd think, getting down those three levels. If gray girl gets her sense together, she would still have to chop through quite a few scabs to get to us. Z, on the other hand, can get through. He knocks scabs aside like he's a miner clearing asteroids—and none are going to stop and mess with him, especially in zero.

There's the ship, Palthaz's baby. Really, a baby. The Zerrek T-15 is the shape of a baby's fat head, with two bulbous cheeks, one giant bulbous forehead, and . . . a disconnected port arm. Must have been hit by another ship in the wrack.

Palthaz's ship is starting to list and drift away. What should have been our port tunnel is a sense-field holding in the atmos, with nothing but space beyond.

Well, I reckon if I just shot a cross in the face, I might have a bit of good luck left.

"Oh no," Kalia says.

"That's the bad hatch, en't it?" I say, pointing to a bit where the running lights flicker irregular under a black handhold. It en't far. About the distance of the main square of Swiney. Not far at all, give or take a few feet of cold dead vacuum.

"Yes. I think so. I don't remember." Kalia's voice trembles. "You can't reach it without a sui—"

"Throw me, Z," I say.

He doesn't hesitate.

Crosses are designed in those vats to take a little punishment. We can hold our breath a good ten minutes. Hard vacuum will kill us, but not so quick. And we can sail through one of the cheap stun-gun sense-fields that Swiney Niney uses to hold back airless space.

Of course I forget to take a good breath when Z hurls me, hard as a blackball, against the field. It shocks me, but I pass right through with only a tingling jolt, and there I am, in shorts and a tank top, sailing like a dumb frozen rock through space.

The cold rips through my skin into my innards. Everything is deep and dark and quiet. Overhead, ships spin away and thrusters blast into vacuum and shards light up the dark, but the crazing has no sound.

My eyes go blurry as the moisture in them freezes. My chest is a giant empty hollow. I can feel my lungs collapsing in on themselves without air.

I sail over the surface of the ship. My first attempt at a handhold fails; my freezing fingers don't clutch fast enough.

My body spins around, and all around me blackness and the lights of Swiney Niney's port, and I'm right near flying past and flying out into the deep black all on my own and I flail and—catch the next handhold.

Hand over hand, on the black frozen plasticene, to that bad hatch, before my insides completely collapse. I'm all over shaking and cramping, and all around me is just darkness and space and horrible silence, and I yank at the hatch, hoping the lock is just plain broken and doesn't need any kind of jury-rigging.

Luck holds. It pops open. A puff of warm oxygen blows out, freezes in the space around me before the autofield engages, keeping atmos in the ship.

I dive right through the field, and I'm tumbling through Palthaz's ship in zero, and it's warm, Starfire bless, and aiya it's full of the sweetest oxygen since Earth was lost.

It takes a minute to find the cockpit and fire it up. A long minute. A minute in which I see the node light up, a few miles out from Swiney, and damned if a real-life Vanguard ship don't come through.

It's big and black, emblazoned with that Resistance symbol, that flame thing. It sends out a heavy barrage of shards. Warning shots for now.

That cross, then—the one killed Quinn, probably the same one killed Cade—she's Vanguard, like Palthaz said. Did I get myself into trouble with the Resistance now?

Swarms of little insect-looking fighters erupt from the belly of the Vanguard ship, blasting bright, big-as-people shards across the black of space at the traffic jam around us. Swiney Niney's collective ships are making for the node, but now that ship's blocking it. They're jostling, swerving, spinning around each other, scraping off circuitry and crashing.

There's two pirate nodes, gone dark, out here in addition to the official one, but not everyone will be able to reach them.

I can.

I bring the ship back around, to dock again. I can see Kalia and Toq and Z, still waiting at the shield. I en't never done a port arm extension, on the fly, hard stop, and this ship flies like a bucket.

Luck? You there?

I take the ship in and throttle back, front thrusters firing, trying for a hard stop.

The port arm grabs my ship's connector. The ship lurches forward, bends the arm, and all the metal around me screeches and groans, and I think for one Imperial minute that I'm about to tear apart the whole dock and send those kids flying into space.

And then the ship lurches the other way, resting back. Luck's there.

We're connected. Z and the kids run into Palthaz's ship, through the bent port arm.

Once they're in the main of the ship I disconnect and dive, down, down. Palthaz's done good work with his big baby of a ship; it maneuvers well around bigger ones. He was smart enough to leave the grav and the enviro controls on manual; those bigger ships are moving slower because of their automated systems; I'm firing only on engine power and making out like a fly from a swatter.

Shard-fire brightens space around us, catches our port arm, blows it to bits, which sends me crashing against the wall, my head bursting with stars for the tenth time today, and I can hardly distinguish my bad vision from the star field outside from the shard-fire. At least I don't have to worry about retracting a bent port arm.

"Wake up!" Toq is shaking me. His face is still a mess of tears. "Please, God! Kalia says she can drive if you just wake—"

"I'm awake." And I can do one thing better than any scab in this burning galaxy.

I reach out, find the node, a connection to the hum and throb of pure space. While all the other ships are scrambling to hit it right, their node-engines roaring and straining, running codes and connections, I bring pure space right to us.

To the paths across black, faster than light and time, out of the fire and death.

"Hang on."

Araskar

It's not going to end with bluebloods, or even humans, not till the whole galaxy goes dark.

I know it's foolish. I know I oughtn't, but here I am, sitting in my quarters, second-guessing myself, overthinking the battle.

I didn't have to send Joskiya. I could have pulled back, or gone myself, or done it on better timing. I keep seeing her, that moment she was scrambling through the mud and that shard turned her head into a pile of meat. I could have gone myself. And the approach! We dropped in too close, but that was because I knew Terracor—knew he would rather use a planet-cracker than target one hot spot. I had to get in there or watch him crack the planet.

And that's a whole other problem. I don't trust my superior. And then there's what the old Marine said.

It's not going to end with bluebloods, or even humans, not till the whole galaxy goes dark. What did he mean by that? Why did an Imperial Marine cross say it?

Sit in your bunk with these kinds of thoughts long enough, and there's nothing to do but take the entire batch of pinks.

My mind quits racing. I can hear the vacuum beyond the ship, a vast emptiness where molecules and atoms float in isolation, sounding their singular pinging notes against a dark hum. I can hear the stars, their nuclear hearts roiling and playing low, thrumming notes that vibrate out through the darkness.

"Secondblade?" The words come swimming out of the blue haze.

I try to move my mouth, but it doesn't work all that well. "Mm."

"Secondblade, are you in there? We've arrived at the rendezvous and it's . . . you need to see."

"Mm." That tongue doesn't quite work at the best of times. I try to get up—doesn't work. I finally find something like words. "Minute."

"Yes, sir." After a moment, "Looks like we're in for a time, Secondblade."

Terracor's going to pull my synthskin tongue right out of my head if he sees me like this. I've got to get up. Doesn't matter if my dumb leg refuses to work. Dumb legs. Neither one is moving. I've got to get up . . .

I don't know how much later it is when someone is banging on my door, and I manage to get enough words out to say, "Give a hand . . ."

It's Helthizor. The kid's been through at least half of what I have, starting on planetfall to Irithessa, and that must be why he doesn't say anything when he comes into my bunk and sees me stoned halfway to the Dark Zone. He puts an arm around me. "Come on, Secondblade," he mutters. "On your feet."

I've never had this kind of comedown before. We stagger through the halls of the ship, him muttering, "You need to look like you're walking, sir," while I keep thinking at my legs to walk, indeed, walk, and they don't do it. Anyone who stops to look gets a glare from Helthizor, and "You have work."

We get outside the bridge, and he whispers, "You've got to move, sir."

"Trying," I mutter. Hey, my fingers flutter. Look at that. I raise my arm a little, and it falls back down. "Trying."

Helthizor sighs, and opens the door onto the bridge.

Terracor spots it immediately. "What's wrong with him?"

"That new leg's not grafting right," Helthizor says. I nod, hoping I look more like a fellow who's suffering from bad synthskin than a half-cooked scab. "What's going on?"

I get a good look at this ecosphere where we're docking. It's a mess. Ships are spinning in space, firing at each other, racing to reach the node. Our gunners fire a round of what were probably meant to be warning shots. A few of them connect.

"Just the usual scabs who hang out in this sort of area," Terracor says. "Our mission was compromised. Public confrontation, and in a place like this, one public confrontation tends to set off another. Who knew that there was a nest of Kurguls trying to move illegal guns right behind our man?" Terracor eyes me. "Stamp your boots, soldier."

I try to bring my hand to my forehead to salute. My fingers move. Progress, aiya?

As we line up to depart the ship, I nod to Helthizor. He nods back. He's a good kid, and owes me his life a couple times over. It's a decent bet that he'll keep quiet. He didn't keep me on the bridge with Terracor long.

I can feel just about every part of me. Good. Arms are tingling, legs appear to be solidly on the ground. I can feel my eyebrows, the roots of the hairs in my skin. That's a funny thing. When was the last time you were aware of your own eyebrows? This is why everyone should try some good drugs. Nobody really appreciates their eyebrows.

The main square of this scummy, sweaty ecosphere is a wreck. A couple of Kurguls are lying dead in the center of it, and shard-marks spread across the concrete buildings, mark the rubble that is thick in the square.

Right in the middle of it all stands Rashiya, leaning over another dead body.

I stumble a bit on my numb feet, and catch myself on Helthizor's shoulder. My slugs all grind to a halt behind me.

"Did you know she was on this mission?" he asks.

My numb tongue matches right up to my numb brain, as I wait, thinking through what to say. "Nobody tells me anything," I slur.

She's frowning as she bends over another body. This one's human. It's a boy, and he's almost got the pale look of those who get a soulsword in their guts. Almost, but there's too much blood for it to have been a soulsword.

"Secondblade." Rashiya looks me straight in the chin. No eye contact for her.

"Lieutenant," I say.

"Not lieutenant anymore," she says, looking back at the body.

"Got promoted?"

"Not really."

Black ops, then. She's taken on some dirty work for Daddy. "Spread out and comb the square, Helthizor."

I nod to him. Not that he needs me to confirm her order. "What happened?"

"This was the target," she says, nudging the boy with her foot. "He confronted me publicly. I wish he had known how much of a mistake it was."

The boy doesn't have the full pale, wispy look of a body that took a soulsword. Looks like Rashiya got a good cut in, but couldn't finish the job. The kid is young. No more than sixteen. Eyes open, cheeks red from tears.

I hate it when they die crying.

Helthizor is calling out positions for our unit. I take the opportunity to grab onto Rashiya's arm. "I believe we owe each other a private briefing."

She points toward one of the concrete warehouses that surround the square—one empty of goods, by the look, with a good portion of the door blown out by shard-fire. "Cozy," I say. We start toward the warehouse—and my legs freeze up, and sound rushes up, a thick, roiling cacophony of notes that falls on my ears like a wall—*till the whole galaxy goes dark*—

"You there, Secondblade?" Rashiya asks.

I lick my lips. "Yeah." It comes out as a mumbling grunt from my bad tongue. I'm cold in this stinking heat. I look up to see her eyes, for the first time. She's actually worried. I half smile, aware of the way the corner of my mouth still won't turn up. "Stamp your boots."

Hell, this is why I take drugs—to avoid nightmares like this.

"Come on," she says. And a moment later, "As long as you're going to be honest."

"I will be if you are."

7

Jaqi

WE COME SCREAMING OUT of pure space, spinning through the black.

"Where are we?" Z says. He unbuckles himself, rises in zero.

He runs his fingers, each one about the thickness of my wrist, over the running lights. Knows his way around a cockpit. Probably could fly this thing, if not navigate. I can tell from how he moves that he's well in zero, which means he's spent a good amount of time in the deep black, where grav is a luxury for full fuel cells.

Look at this hidden depth to Zaragathora, Eater of Flesh. Kills and—does other things!

"Are we far from the ecosphere?" Kalia asks.

"We're nowhere." This is a nice chunk of nothing, empty of everything except ghosts. The star field is distant pinpricks, all around, above and below, except for the wide black blotch of the Dark Zone. "This is why I'm good company, kids. There's no fixed nodes anywhere near here, no hints to our location. I dropped you right on the big ass of nowhere. Good spot, when there's trouble."

Kalia and Toq don't speak. Poor kids. Still in shock.

"Why here?" Z says. "We're burning fuel."

"If I know Palthaz, it's been a while since he ran a basic diagnostic." And he probably never learned the trick of routing through med-grade bacterial fiber to save on said fuel. "We need a second before we go . . . on."

Where's on, Jaqi?

That takes a minute to figure out. After that minute, it takes another minute.

I'm going to have to take them to Bill's. He knows everything in wild space. He's probably got the line on this kill order from the Vanguard. If there's one spot in the wild worlds even the Vanguard couldn't find, it's Bill's.

They'll be safe, and I can get out of this grim and back to that business of living a real life.

I flip open a panel on the ceiling, revealing the grav controls. "Who's in the mood for some gravity?" My guess is that these kids haven't been running in the deep black long; they were raised planetside, and they're going to need a few good hours of grav a day to keep healthy.

"I peed my pants," Toq says. "I was too scared to hold it."

"That's okay," I say. "I would have peed my pants too."

"Why?" Toq says. "Were you scared?"

"Enough for my heart to burst," I say. "But they make crosses so we don't pee under stress. We're supposed to be perfect soldiers."

"I peed too," Kalia says, after a moment.

"Palthaz must have some spare clothes around here." They both look ready to cry. Damn. Bring some funny, Jaqi. Cheer these ones up. "How about you?" I ask Z. "Did you hold it? Or are you Zaragathora, Pee-er of Pants?"

The kids chortle. Z frown-snarls. So far, he's about as funny as a constipated Imperial officer.

"I will find clothes," he says. "Are you hitting the gravity or not?"

"Hold your pee, Z," I say. Both of the kids giggle again. Hey, look at that. Not crying. I switch on the gravity and Z is knocked down into his seat. They laugh again.

Palthaz's gravity is special nasty, making me feel like a cat's scratching the top of my head. Probably just repurposed an old shock field generator. I've heard—not that I've ever been planetside, not since I was too small to remember—that planetside gravity feels nice, natural, not like this skin-busting itchy pressure, and not even like the ecospheres. Kalia and Toq's expressions tell me this is true.

"I don't like this," Toq says. "I think we would rather float. Palthaz let us float on the way here."

Polite kid. I unbuckle them. "You need some grav, or you'll get the bends once you get planetside again."

"What does that mean?"

"We should just do what she says, Toq," Kalia says. "She knows about spaceships."

Z comes back with clothes. Looks like Palthaz had some extra packed for them. Toq starts pulling off his wet pants. He looks at me and Z for a minute, as if deciding whether he can strip in front of us. Kalia pulls Toq into the room right behind the cockpit—Palthaz's cabin, I figure—and says, "Sorry! We'll change in here!"

I look at Z. "Bluebloods, eh? I guess they can afford to be embarrassed about their starks."

"The dead boy has spare clothes, as well," Z says. "If you want to change, they will fit you."

Takes me a minute to realize what he's saying. Quinn. The damn kid who died because he thought he was helping me. I knew him for about two hours, and I figure he was the bravest soul in the galaxy.

"They won't like seeing me in their dead brother's raggy."

"Their brother died well," Z says. "You would honor him by wearing his clothes."

"You're an odd scab, anyone ever tell you?"

He stands a bit closer, and the hot, stinking breath from between his sharp teeth is almost as bad as the skin-prickles from Palthaz's cheap-ass gravity. "You promised pay."

"You'll find money in your hand soon enough," I say. "Just make yourself useful."

"You will pay me," he says, "when we get where we are going."

"All right, all right, just breathe in the other direction." I shove him away gently, hoping he doesn't rip me in half for it. "Why do you need money so evil? Don't tell me you got into pit fighting to help your poor sick mother."

He holds his peace, long enough that I actually look in his big red eyes, surrounded by that stark white skin and black curling tattoos. He's looking out the porthole at the starless patch of the Dark Zone.

"It is for my people," he says. "We are fighting our own war, against the corrupt rulers who stole our land."

"Oh, right. You know, this trip really needed more believers."

———————

Araskar

"You first," she says.

I, with great pride in my levelheadedness, avoid pointing out her hypocrisy: tell me everything, and I'll tell you nothing. "You deserve the truth, Rash."

"If you're here to tell me about how you were out of your head, save it."

"I wasn't out of my head yet." I ease myself onto a slab of concrete. You would think this place was uninhabited, given that only corpses and Vanguard are filling the square. Quiet, too, other than the subtle buzz of the engines, and the chatter of the animals in the woods. I wonder what sort of magical fun we'll run into out in the wild there. No doubt there's enough contraband to make up for the pinks I just finished off.

Not the time to think of that. I focus on Rashiya. She looks older already. Funny, that. It's barely been a month.

"So, I've never told anyone this, but I used to have a little . . . habit."

She doesn't speak. That's good, I think. I've got her attention.

"On Irithessa, I wasn't trying to die," I say.

"You told those Kurguls to kill you."

"True." I had forgotten about that. "I didn't go looking for death, Rash. I went looking for drugs."

She nods, still facing away from me. "I hoped you would tell me."

"You know?"

She nods. "Helthizor."

"That little shit." I suppose it's too much to ask that people would keep their mouths shut. "Just now?"

"He's known for a while, Araskar. Said he didn't know who else to tell, and he was afraid of what Terracor might do to you. They need you."

"He's got no right to tell you that."

"You have no right to endanger your life like this."

"Brain bullets never killed anyone," I snap.

"No, just made them stupid and slow and got them killed in the field. You think I've never seen this before? You think you're the first soldier that did this?"

I really don't want to hear about other sad-case soldiers like me. "You and little Helthizor have nothing to worry about. I quit a while ago. The supply ran out, and it seemed like a good time."

She turns back to me. It's funny, but sometimes a little thing can make a war-hardened soldier turn into a kid. The way she looks at me, I remember that she's spent a lot of the last few years with her father at risk. I suppose when you know your pater's chopped head could show up on the news, it makes you look at life a little different. "You need to promise me that's the truth."

It's in the orbit of truth. I didn't plan to quit but . . . why not? "My word of honor, for what that's worth."

"Worth enough to me," she says softly.

"Now it's your turn," I say. "I want truth about this mission. Hell, about consolidation in general." I motion toward the body. "Young, for a kill. Start with him."

"There's an intel leak, going as high as my father's inner circle, and as far back as Irithessa."

"I heard. That intel got twelve of my best killed on Keil's moon," I say. "Terracor was willing to crack a moon open for it.

And you're stuck here in the shits of space, killing kids for it? What leaked?"

She sits next to me. "That, I haven't asked. My father doesn't tell me everything. High-level leak, and the kids have it, and we're supposed to recover it."

"I suspect he tells you more than he tells us."

"You'd be surprised." I can't tell if she's lying.

This air tastes awful. Feels like I have to chew it. I would evil like to get back to Irithessa, where there's real atmos. I suppose it's too much to ask that I could breathe good air now and then. "Are we back on the mission together?"

"For now," she says. She rubs at a patch of synthskin, a piece of her head that's been repaired. It's taken a hit recently, a good hit. Her neutral gray getup is hiding a personal shield, I can tell, so it must have been quite a shot. She peels away the half-melted synthskin from her forehead, rolls it into a ball, tosses it on the ground. "That's sloppy work."

"You should see this leg," I say. "Had it all rebuilt on the fly after Keil, and it's barely one step up from a peg."

"That'll make it even easier to knock you on your ass," she says.

"Oh, your day is coming in the ring, young Miss Starfire." I tap my soulsword hilt. "One of these days, the practice blade comes for you."

"Don't call me Miss Starfire ever again."

"Tell me the truth about all this. Consolidation. What's it really about?"

She looks at me like I'm stupid. "About making a government that could last."

"It's not about killing humans?"

She laughs. "You think we could kill every human in the

galaxy? Three trillion sentients?"

"That number's gone down of late," I say. "Look, every-one—Terracor, all the other superiors—they're not talking like this is about intel. I heard plenty of folks—" I stop myself from mentioning her pater. *The human stain.*

"Of course," she says. "You don't go telling the spaceways that you've got an intel leak."

"They're talking," I say, "like it's about humans. Not blue-bloods. But humans."

She shrugs. "I can't blame anyone for hating humans, not after what we've been through."

"We been through as much as we could expect," I say.

"Three trillion humans in the galaxy. Since the founding of the Second Empire, at least six times as many crosses went to death in the Dark Zone."

"Okay, so it's about . . ."

"It's about intel. I think it's about time that we get back to finding it." She turns back to the doorway.

"So," I say, getting to my feet. "See you in the ring?"

She doesn't answer. And I stumble out into the grating filtered sunlight of this ecosphere, for what I have just pronounced my first day sober. Everything stinks.

8

Jaqi

"**WHAT WERE YOUR PARENTS** like, Jaqi?" Kalia asks. She and Toq are sitting at the table, their seats bolted into the wall of the common area, which, as common areas go on tiny spaceships, is almost designed for humans. Seats around the triangular space, a good five paces across. A couple of games and books in a latching cabinet that the kids have popped open. Protein packs open, and the smell makes my stomach rumble and makes me sick at the same time. I sit down and take a bite.

It tastes almost as bad as I smell.

Z and I finished the diagnostic an hour ago, having been up in the guts of the ship a good day, checking all the lines and the cells, emptying the acid dumps, starting new cultures growing on the batteries, and it's hot and nasty in there, and you've got to grease up with anti-oxitate, no matter how it burns your skin. After the full diagnostic, a girl gets tired, aiya, and ready for at least a cleaning-field when there's no water for a bath. So I found the cleaning-field and turned the thing on, and didn't get a damn thing except a few sparks. Should have run a diagnostic on that while I was at it.

I guess I'll get clean at Bill's. For now, I smell about the worst that anything's ever smelled in the galaxy. Except for Z.

"Jaqi?"

"I told you about my folks back on Swiney, didn't I?"

The girl and her brother have a couple of books spread out on the table. The boy is looking at the pictures, and moving his hands along the words under the pictures, making the sounds with his mouth.

Wonder if the letters go all fuzzy on him too. Wish I could ask.

Kalia says, "I mean like . . . did they take you to the beach, or did they like to go flying, or . . ."

I think she's joking. She must be. Go flying? Like, for fun? In a spaceship? Who gets in a cramped little recycled-air rustrider for fun? I guess she's just trying to talk instead of think about her dead brother. And dead dad. Poor kid.

"They worked, mostly," I say. "My mother liked to sing. She would sing me to sleep at night."

"Oh, I heard about that," she says. "Yeah, you can tell when a cross goes wrong because they like music. The vats are supposed to grow crosses that don't really like art or music or anything that will distract them from fighting. Crosses that sing or that make music or draw are supposed to go back into the vats."

"How'd you know that? Your pater?"

"No," she says. "I read it in a book."

Books. I try not to sound stupid. "There's a, um, book about that?"

"There's lots. I had to read about it for school, but that was just propaganda about how the crosses want to fight. My dad gave me a book by a guy who joined the Resistance. *My Private Vat.* Did you ever read that?"

"No, don't figure I did." If we keep talking about books, I'm going to look evil foolish. "You ever—"

She starts right in lecturing. "It's all about aberrations. The

Jorians that escape, and have kids, and how crosses are people and they all live in fear, and it says that this has been happening ever since the beginning. I guess after the Fall, when all the original Jorians died, the elite families had this big cloning project to bring the original Jorians back. That's where the vats came from. But it was corrupted. First the original Jorians couldn't be replicated, then they mixed the DNA with human to make crosses. The guy who wrote the book, he knows a lot because he's a cross and he traveled with crosses. You know?"

"Oh, right." What in five suns is the Fall? Does everyone who reads books talk like this?

I figure my confusion must be visible, because she starts explaining some more. "So I guess there's like, five parts of history. For humans, anyway, and you're kind of human. There's Earth. There's the Alliance, which is when humans and Jorians joined together to make the nodes between the old galaxy and here. There's the First Empire. And then there's the Fall and the Chaos. When the old galaxy died and its stars were scattered."

"You're talking about church," Toq says. "Church is boring."

"Quiet, Toq. God hears when you say stuff like that, you know." She bites her lip. "And there's the Second Empire. And I guess . . . I guess the Second Empire is over, now. We're in the sixth part of history for humans."

Yeah, part six is probably going to be titled *The Part Where All the Humans Died.* "Your pater, he, uh, he made crosses, though. Did you tell him you read about how it's wrong, and all?"

"Oh, yeah. Dad gave me the book. He told me that he stopped sending the aberrations back to be melted down. He thought the Resistance had the right idea; our whole church had like, secret meetings for people who agreed with the Resistance. He let Quinn in. I listened at the door." She smiles. "I know that he started shipping his crosses secretly to the Resistance. At least the aberrations. He said that he had to keep selling some crosses to the Empire, or they would come for him, but . . ." She nervously turns the pages of one of her books. "The Resistance came for him instead."

Z walks in. He's given up on finding something that fits; he's just got a towel wrapped around his middle, which I guess is close enough, considering he was just wearing synth-scale trousers before.

"Turn off this damn gravity," he says. It's *almost* not a snarl.

"I was just starting not to notice it," I say. I'm used to scratchy grav fields in cheap ships.

"I want to float," Toq says. "Can we turn it off?"

"Yeah, the gravity itches me," Kalia says, in that tone that's still a bit snooty. All I need now is for her to sniff and mutter, *Something must be done,* like one of those old ladies in the dramas. Nice girl, though, no matter how big a catch her pater had. And a church girl! I en't never met someone who went to a real church, and talked about a God and all.

"What were you talking about?" Z says. "The book. About vats."

"*My Private Vat,*" Kalia says. "Did you read it?"

"Yes," he says. "The author wrote another. About indigenous peoples and Imperial domain. *Our Blood, Our Land, Our Hell.* Every sentient should read it."

Him too? I'm surrounded by a bunch of book bugs?

Kalia's looking at me. Like she's checking my skin for a tick. I want to ask her what she sees. Then she speaks.

She says, "I can teach you to read, Jaqi. I taught Toq."

"I . . ." Well, burning hell and the devil. "How did you know?"

She doesn't tell me. She just says, all evil nice, "I want to teach you. It's fun. Our nanny didn't do a good job of teaching Toq, and Quinn wasn't very patient with him . . ." She gets a bit quiet at her brother's name, and comes back with ". . . so I did."

It's one of the nicest things anyone's offered me in a while, anyway. "Like, what he's doing? You point at the word and then you make the sound?"

"Yes," Toq says. "Look! This says 'elephant.'"

He shows me the little markings on his page, like I'm going to understand it too. As far as I can tell, those little markings could be a recipe for chocolate cake—damn, this protein pack tastes terrible—but I smile and say, "Does it now?"

"Reading is fun," Kalia said. "Toq even likes it, even though he's just learning. Did your parents know how to read?"

"Maybe?" I shrug. Might as well be honest, now the airlock's open on my secrets. "They might've had a data dump for it, but had we no time for reading in the spaceways. If we went into mid-galaxy, we might get force-drafted."

Oh hell, she's going to cry again. "I'm so sorry."

"En't nothing to be sorry about. Every life's got its share of scabs." I touch her face. She's thinking about her brother, I can tell. "Hey. We're gonna get you safe, in well."

"I want answers from the children," Z snaps. Aiya, he can kill a mood. "Why does the Vanguard want you two so badly?"

"I don't know," Kalia says.

"Quinn said you were getting out of known space," I say. "I don't know how you were supposed to do that."

"This." She taps something and I recognize it, and realize she's been hanging on to it. It's that black box they were carrying on Swiney. "It's not just for hiding us. It's got a star map, but it's encrypted. Um . . ." Her eyes are tearing up. I put an arm around her. "Quinn knew the encryption code."

I hug her close. Damn, we'd better hope that gray-wearing Vanguard bitch didn't get anything out of Quinn's head with her sword.

Z reaches for the black box. "May I see?" He lifts it up without their answer, peers at it closely. The thing's fancier than I thought at first. Little scrolls and curls go along the sides; might be some kind of writing, for those who know lots of kinds of writing.

He lets out a long, slow breath. I can smell it even over my fishy clothes. "This is old," he says. "Jorian writing, Second Era. I've seen the like in a museum. Where did you get this?"

"Dad had it," Kalia said.

"You've been to a museum?" I ask. Z is starting to make me look like the savage.

"Suits can decrypt this," Z says.

"Aiya. That means you have to deal with Suits."

"What are Suits?" Kalia asks.

Z's frowning. A real frown, but not a scowl. "Where are we going?"

"A dark node, and yes, there's Suits there."

"Why, exactly, did this node go dark?"

"It's Bill's," I say. "It's safe."

"Nothing's safe," Z says.

Will he never stop killing the mood?

9

Jaqi

WE COME SPINNING OUT of pure space to Bill's.

My head is hurting; I've been up a good thirty-six hours now, and I still couldn't stomach more than a couple bites of protein. I asked Z to drive at one point, but he said he en't piloted one of these before, and he wasn't going to risk us on the drop from pure space in case we hit a gas storm world, or atmos ... and I figure that was a comment on my navigating skills, and I tell you, this guy is going to take some getting used to, aiya. If he wasn't so big, I would have slapped him sore.

Bill's place looms up before us.

"Oh my gosh," Kalia says.

"What's a gosh?" I ask.

She doesn't answer. Her eyes are glued ahead of us. I gotta admit, it's a sight.

Bill's started out as a couple of hidey-holes in an asteroid. The original lump of rock still sits at the heart, but since he got it, he's added two concentric rings, alight with tiny flickering flames from thrusters, turning the apparatus. The rings are obviously cobbled together; circuits and wires and scrap metal and component girders stuck to plasticene sprayed from the hose, dried in lumps as big as our ship. He's added more raw rock; other asteroids to make a kind of spiderweb of girders and plasticene. Normally he uses the other rocks as guest quarters, or storage, but everything's dark, no running lights; I'm guessing only the central quarters are even running atmos.

Bill's got an impressive setup, especially for how it's cobbled together. But that's not what's drawing Kalia's eye.

See, the running lights of Bill's are the *only* light in the sky.

Behind us, the star field spreads out, the pale ribbon of the galaxy running through it. And behind Bill's, the dark patch of sky—stretching as far as you can see. No stars, nothing.

"You didn't— That's the Dark Zone!"

"It's how he keeps quiet," I say. "No one goes hunting old nodes on the edge of the Dark Zone."

"The Navy surely campaigns here," Z says.

"En't so. The Navy has nodes inside the Dark Zone they use to attack. Had nodes." I remember what Quinn said. "Now they're stuck in there forever." The kids are staring like the Dark Zone's about to come alive and eat them. "Don't worry. It won't hurt you. On thrusters, it would still take you decades just to touch the edge of that." It's always given me the creeps, especially the way that dark patch has grown over the years. But then, I got used to it. This was my home.

My parents left me at Bill's when they had nowhere else to go. Eleven years ago. Too dangerous to take me when they shipped out, on a rat-scow, illegally scavenging through trash for repurposing material. Or that's what Bill told me. They never came back.

It en't a subject I'm fond of. I used to think they died a noble death, or maybe they was still out there. Now I know that the Imperial Fleet most likely saw that rat-scow clinging to the side of their garbage dump, and shot it right off like a bug, killing all the rats, including my parents. Heroic, en't it? All odds on, my folks died sifting trash.

I grew up in the hallways of this asteroid, back when Bill had nasty old grav that hardly worked. These days the rings turn it all fast enough that there's a bit of real grav in there, the kind they can generate in ecospheres. Fancy.

"Oh my gosh!" There's that gosh again, from Kalia. What is this gosh thing? Name of the blueblood god? "What *is* that?"

Toq screams and grabs my arm.

And that's their first view of a Suit.

This Suit has five human arms, clad in steelskin. Five arms, like he's collected them up off the ground.

The arms sprout from a platform running with light and wires, which is wired to a metal girder that connects to the lumps of wires and circuit boards and pistons running from the helmeted head—and then on the other side, another girder arm that ends in another bunch of real flesh arms. Try to imagine replacing your fingers with small arms. You can't see the face under the dark helmet, and that I am mighty thankful for. If the Suits don't give you the creeps, you might be a creep your own self.

The old Empire mapped out the entire galaxy and stuck nodes everywhere they could, to keep trade flowing without the need for Jorians to constantly navigate. In the millennia since, lots of nodes have gone dark, the codes lost, the pure-space wormhole simply unused.

The Suits find the old nodes. That's why you need them, out here in the wild. They are the only scabs in the galaxy who can get nodes working again, by running every code they can collect in every bit of old tech in every scrapyard in every system in the stars. For Suits, though, "tech" don't distinguish between squishy parts and metal. They all start out organic, and they start cutting themselves up, trading organs and limbs for tech until they turn into evil scary hybrids. They splice brains into their databases, pulling out everything that has a fragment, a memory, a clue as to the tech they're looking for.

This Suit leaps away from the ring in front of us, floats along the spindle arm of the metal ring. "It's telling Bill we're coming."

"That's gross," Kalia says. "That's really gross."

Toq makes a little whine and clutches my arm harder.

"No arguing with you there," I say.

"Who's in the asteroid? More of . . . more of those?"

"Hope not," I say. "No, just a rough, with one hand on a gun and the other picking his nose." Toq doesn't giggle. I thought it was a good one.

Z's watching the asteroid as it gets closer. "This does not seem like a place of profit."

"Bill's pulled through all the custom in the wild. Just calm yourself down."

Araskar

Withdrawal is indeed a bitch.

The shaking and the sweats didn't last too long. My legs and arms keep going numb, but that I can deal with. The real bitch is, the drugs are all I can think about. A couple of those brain bullets, and I will sink into the music. Two pink pills, and I could hear the sweet, stirring strings of a nebula. I could hear the roiling, thunderous beat within the heart of a star. I could feel it stir me, embrace me, and I would forget this mission.

Instead I get to hear Swiney Niney's chatter. Animals, probably illegal minor crosses, in the jungle, chattering. Bugs. Dripping water. Mosquitoes buzzing in my ears. And Helthizor, muttering under his breath. "We're way off time."

"We're going the right way," I say. "Relax. No one's shooting at us."

"I wish you would tell me what's on your mind," he says. "I'm supposed to be advising you."

"Emperor Turka wished he could shit without a winch to open his asshole, and look where that got him."

Helthizor looks back over the crew behind us before he turns back and whispers, "You feeling any better, Secondblade?"

He's about as sly as a supernova. "I quit."

"Good."

"Watch your tone, Helthizor." My leg is seizing up and going numb. My arm feels too heavy with that gun in it, too. My head is throbbing. It wants to be filled with the music instead of the shitty muck of this ecosphere. "You talk to me, not Rashiya, you understand?"

I expect deferment, or something high-headed, but he just says, "I was worried."

My destination is at the top of the Swiney Niney hill. It's the only other color in the jungle green. A thin, crystalline Jorian-built structure, all twisting spires and domes once made to shine in the sun. Now painted solid black. And hung on the gates, a black, enormous skull.

"A Necro temple?" Helthizor says when it comes into view. "I can't see them reacting well to all of us."

"That, Helth," I say, "is why the company is moving on.

I will take this myself." He doesn't respond, so I say, "Now, Sergeant. I won't be long. We all go in there together, we'll spook 'em."

"Is this another stupid risk?"

"Aren't they all?" I try to give him a big grin. "Have fun in the woods. Find me a pet monkey. Always wanted one."

I don't bother to wait around for what he's going to say. I've got too much to think on right now as it is. I walk to the entrance of the entirely cheerful Necro temple. You wouldn't think there were so many decorative skulls in this part of the wild worlds.

"Death!" I say as enthusiastically as I can to the skull. "Death!"

It isn't hard. I sure feel like death.

The gates open.

The Necro temple is the biggest, fanciest building in this shithole. That's not saying much. I've seen pictures, in two, three, and four dimensions, of the one on Irithessa. It takes up its own private island, towers half a mile into the sky, and Necron devotees from all over the galaxy come to learn about the glories of not-living. Then they go out into the wide galaxy, to scream "Death!" at sporting events, and hand out annoying pamphlets in spaceports.

That's what folks think, anyway. They also run the best black market this side of lost Earth. There's an astonishing number of Kurguls, minor drones from the big nests, who decide to take up a life in service of the Necro-Lord. Religious tax exemption is just the start of the benefits.

The yard of the temple is filled with remnants of dead things. Bones from animals. Drying strips of hide, still bloody, stretched across sticks in the yard. I nearly trip over them, still stumbling over my tingling leg. It's my good leg going numb, too. That just isn't fair.

A cloud of insects soars up into my face. Flies as big as my thumb, right in the eyes. I raise my hand to swat one out of the air.

"Don't do that."

The Necro priest has had his face altered. He might have been a Kurgul once, by his squat frame, four and a half feet at the tallest, if he cut the tentacles off his face. Or he might have been a human, for all I know, if he chopped off his nose. I can't see his eyes to tell. His face is almost a perfect skull, with that empty inverted V of a nose and little black eyes set in sunken eye sockets. Tattoos fester his bare, bulging forehead. He's clothed in a mass of black that looks like he might have made a deal with some sentient cloth, just to get a big scary cloak. He raises his hand and the flies come to land on his arm, like falcons returning to their master.

"Salutes. I'm Araskar."

"I know, Vanguard. You've caused a lot of trouble." A thin red tongue emerges from between those bare teeth and licks them. "A lot of death. And you carry a weapon for your own death. Presumptuous."

He's looking at my waist, where my short soulsword—really just a knife—sits, waiting for the moment I dishonor myself enough to use it. "I know your lord pretty well by now, I think."

"Presumptuous." He turns and goes inside.

Inside, the incense hits just a bit thicker than the stink of the air. Suppose if you're constantly sacrificing animals and stripping their hides, things can get a bit smelly, even for this shithole. The inside of the temple is dim, only lit by phosphor candles, throwing reflective, dancing light everywhere. The smoke bugs my eyes, makes them water, but hey, why complain about that when my twitchy body is screaming for drugs?

An adept scurries around like a bug, his head down, cloaked.

On the table, there is a very large dead thing. As far as crazing crosses go, it's a work of art, a mishmash of humanoid components and insect, with four mandibles emerging from the sides of its head. Two burly legs clad in black boots emerge from the tail, and a massive stinger thrusts up, glistening with venom, from the chest. Someone put all the parts in strange places.

"That was our NecroWasp," says the priest.

"I'm sorry for your loss," I say.

"We will repair it. It is dead, and it was dead, and it will fight for Death."

I raise my hand, showing him the steel scrip of the letter of credit. The candles make pinpricks of light off the surface. "I need information."

He laughs, low and loud. "That's not worth anything, not until the galaxy's settled down. Since Irithessa fell, hard matter only. Or codes for dark nodes, what the Suits trade in. Have any of those?"

"Afraid not." I didn't think that would work anyway. I step forward. "I made a nice offering to your boss. And I'm not afraid to do it again."

That tongue goes over those teeth again. It reminds me of a worm scurrying over rocks. "I would love to join our Lord in glorious death."

"Oh, walk out the airlock." Religious types. "I just want answers."

The adept comes closer, mixing a bucketful of some stinking slop. Something black, and stinking, and probably organic. He's painting the NecroWasp's body with the stuff. I catch him looking at me.

Old to be a Necro adept. A Zu-Path, chubby face, with those warty growths, and an eye patch.

"Perhaps we will take your credit," the priest says, suddenly. "Come with me. I will attempt to answer your questions."

"Hold on." I grab the adept's arm. He yanks it away from me, digs in his cloak for a gun, but the priest pulls his own piece out almost as fast as I draw my soulsword.

The priest trains his gun on me. "I would hate to offer you to our Lord without the ceremonial preparations. Please leave."

"You stink worse than the rest of this hole," I tell the Zu-Path. "You hiding from something?"

The shards in the priest's gun hum. The Zu-Path eyeballs my sword. The priest mutters something inaudible through his teeth.

"Come on, you've got that nice soul you don't want to lose," I say.

"I don't know a thing," he says. "I'm just trying to stay out of the way of—you types."

I don't know about that. He chose to come in here, not hiding, and he's eyeballing that letter of credit. It takes top-quality-vat balls to approach someone who would kill to get to you.

"He is an adept of Death," the priest says, "and that is all you need to know."

I take a chance on asking the Zu-Path words. "Formoz of Keil. You know him?"

"You could say that." The Zu-Path's one eye flashes back and forth from me to the priest's gun. "He was liquidating. Offering a couple billion to anyone willing to shuttle his kids off Keil to the wild worlds. I heard about it through—through a fella I know. There was a whole network of us in on it. I was supposed to pass the kids off here. Waited for my contact for an evil time—at least a few days past deadline. Then I heard you was involved—you Vanguard. I took a walk, and when I got back, my ship and catch were gone!"

"Adept!" The priest looks angry now; that is, if you can read expressions in that skull of a face. "You are to forget these things, in the service of Death!"

"Ignore him," I say. "How'd you get out?"

"I left them with a cross," he said. "Dumb girl. Short, dark skin. Just a navigator. I was going back for them—really was—when you arrived and everything went nuts and now they've stolen my ship and I en't seen a dime."

The priest is muttering something, louder now. Sounds like a prayer—has that kind of singsong, repeated cadence.

"This girl—where'd she take them?"

"Don't know."

"If I stick you with my soulsword, will it agree?"

His one eye opens about wide enough to make two eyes. "She's from Bill's. Probably took them back there. It's a dark node, just this side of Sector 118-R, right up next to the Dark Zone—"

The priest fires. Shards flash right by my hand, and blow that one-eyed Zu-Path head and most of the torso apart.

I am left holding a sad, fat little arm, with no body to match it.

The priest exhales. "I would have done that sooner, but I must have prayer to prepare for the sacrifice. As it is, our Necrotic Lord is not pleased with you, Vanguard." He cocks his head at me. "You have your information. I have a price for you to pay."

"Oh, yeah?" I wave the arm at him. "It doesn't seem to me you helped much in my information gathering."

"Our Necrotic Lord would, most likely, have forgiven me if I had just shot the adept to start with." He smiles, about as creepy a smile as mine was when my face melted off. "Lucky for you I am a devoted servant, and I took the time to pray while you two chatted."

"Fair enough." This priest is a bit wiser than he lets on. "You want the letter of credit, then?"

"No. I want you to make an offering. A great and noble offering to Death." He points to the massive stinking NecroWasp. "For it is dead, and was dead, and now it shall fight for death."

When I understand what he means, I groan. This is what I get for saying I wanted a pet.

10

Jaqi

EN'T BUT TEN MINUTES after we've landed, hugged, taken the kids to where they can get a bath, and Z too, that Bill turns to me and yells, "What the burning hell is wrong with you?"

Bill looks older. He's lost every little bit of his hair, and so his head is glistening in the pale and flickering light of the overheads. Or maybe they en't flickering. Maybe that's just his head shaking. He looks angrier, too. Not the usual.

"Those are wanted kids! Haven't you heard?"

"I've been too busy running for my life." To which I add, "Hell of a way to greet me, Bill."

"I en't in the mood for hugs and kisses, Jaqi! I en't a cross. The galaxy's your playground now, not mine." His big old chin sticks out, prominently displaying the flash-burns that he's had there since I can remember. "I taught you better than to come running to me every time you need something."

I stand there just trying to think through this. I didn't know anywhere else to go than Bill's.

Bill groans, breaking the silence. "God, I need a beer. And en't no beer come through in a month, because we went dark. Until you got here!"

"I might have beer in the ship. I en't searched all the matter on there." I try to smile.

"Guarantee you searched it, miss eats-every-damn-thing-in-the-station."

He still knows me.

The overheads glow, as usual, flickering, casting gray shadows and washing out everyone's faces. The ceiling is too low, low enough that Z has to duck. The main area boasts a couple of old smelly chairs, a long wooden table, a shelf with some games, and Bill's prize possession, his guitar. In another room, simulated sunshine on a few sick-looking plants. This is Bill's. Big, cold, with bad lighting. Home.

"Bill, it en't me needs something, it's these kids! Your place is safe. Always has been. So safe even a fart can't escape, ai?" I try a smile.

"I ought to kick you out of the airlock."

"Might be worth it, to get away from your farts."

His mask breaks for a moment. "I checked with one of them doctors. A real one. Had the card and all. He says there en't nothing wrong with my guts." And then back to anger, as if he's remembering he can't afford to smile. "Jaqi, there's a kill order on humans."

"I heard. On bluebloods, and I guess merchants too."

"All humans. Even swine like me."

"Oh. The crosses—the Vanguard—they want to kill every single burning human in the whole burning galaxy?"

"That's the chatter. The scabs of the galaxy're calling it the Red Peace." He holds up a hand. "Red like blood, human blood, is."

"I get it."

"There's chatter coming in from all over, specifically about them kids. Must be a hell of a catch for you to risk yourself like this."

"No," I say, "en't no catch. They're just little kids in trouble." I don't say *their brother got himself killed, for me.*

"What am I supposed to do with them?"

"You know the wild worlds a lot better than I do, Bill. Come on now." He don't say a thing. "You can't leave them with me—I'll get drunk and leave them in a bar. Or some crazing." It's damn silent, except for the hum of the atmos cycling in, and the faint crying of the kids.

"Bill?"

He shakes his head.

I guess I figured Bill was going to take over. I tell him so. "Bill, you're going to have to pack up if there's Vanguard after all humans. Take the kids with you. Make a deal with some Kurguls. Get a hidey-hole on a wild world, so far from everything the Vanguard won't find you."

"Jaqi, the Vanguard are running all around the Empire, and soon the wild worlds, hacking folk up with those soulswords, sucking up every bit of memory they can. They'll find us. You weren't the only scab on Niney that knew my place. I don't know where I'm going to hide. There en't a scab in the wild worlds won't sell me out with these kids in tow."

He sinks down into his chair. It lets out a sigh, and a little cloud of dust from the cushion.

I know the chair Bill's sitting in. I helped him weld it out of scrap metal, glue in the fabric and the stuffing, helped him sew up the edges. It's a decent chair. If you're going to sit at a table with a bunch of scabs like to shoot you any minute, might as well keep your butt cozy.

For that matter, I tasted ice cream at this table, my first time. It had gone hard and dry in vacuum, but I felt like a princess eating it. I cooked with Bill whenever we could get real matter, although he never shared his cheese (that being the main cause of those farts. Nothing wrong with his guts, my half-Jorian ass). He even bought me a doll once, off a trader who'd raided a big family catch. I wore it to pieces, and when it ripped beyond repair, we held a little funeral and shot it into space.

"And what are you going to do? You coming with us? I could use a cross, even if you en't exactly muscle."

"I . . ."

He's waiting on an answer. "Come on, Jaqi."

Well, shit.

My thoughts never went further than here. I'd explain the problem with the little ones, and let Bill take it. If I run with Bill and the kids to the wild worlds, that means . . . that means no Irithessa and plays and fancy lovefolk and no fancy restaurants.

I just want to live.

"Hell, Bill, I . . ."

"I see." He shakes his head. "I don't blame you, Jaqi." After a moment he stands up. He don't put an arm around me, or anything like that, but he sounds a little choked up. "I was real juiced for you. I heard the Resistance had won. Heard that a cross, Mister John Starfire by name, was sitting on the throne on Irithessa. I figured, one day, ten, twenty years down, she'll come back and she'll be fat and smiling and have a passel of babies. Never hear another stupid thing out of your mouth. Figured you'd write one of them books about your life of crime. Fancy people like those things."

Me write a book? I laugh at that. "Some dreams, Bill."

"You're a smarter girl than you know," he says. "Damn, Jaqi, I en't got a place to go."

"The kids got some fancy bit of Jorian matter," I say. "Say it's going to help them get out of known space."

"Out of the galaxy? You listening to more fables?"

"The girl, she told me, said that once the old Jorians used to run between galaxies. We'll figure it out once we can get a Suit to hack this thing the kids have. It's got information, Bill."

"Crazing," Bill says.

"Come see what they got," I say. I'm hoping that Bill, as soft-hearted as he can be, will kin to the kids like I have, maybe get his brain working when he sees how alone they are. "We're safe for now."

———

Araskar

A dark node, just this side of Sector 118-R, where the Dark Zone begins. Bill's place.

I watch the priest pump his NecroWasp full of sticky green synthblood. Everyone should see something like this in their life, if only to put them off food forever. He's wheeled in a big tank full of the stuff, and hooked up a massive pump to a couple of spots on the Wasp. As it pumps, he prays, and finally, with one grand "Death!" of an amen, the thing starts to move.

"So, no need for cash?"

"Honor our Necrotic Lord." The priest rubs the NecroWasp's shoulder. "Bring this into battle. Let it pay tribute in your Red Peace."

"How loyal is this thing?" I ask.

"Loyal to death."

The NecroWasp blinks its segmented eyes.

"Ah, there's one other question for you," I say, and I hate myself as soon as the words come out of my mouth. "There's some matter I've been seeking. Contraband."

Had he anything like a human face, I would say this priest is raising his eyebrow. As it is, it's just thin white skin rearranging itself above his sunken black eye. "Well, war hero. We wouldn't want to deny your noble self."

I put my hand on my soulsword. "Get me some pinks, you scabby corpse, or you'll never get to die."

The priest coughs in surprise, turns around, and scurries off to the back. The Necros are supposed to have religious exemption from dying on the end of a soulsword. Good way to scare them.

Just a couple more pinks, then I can go back on a fast. I probably won't need but one. I can even spread them out. Once a week. That's a nice, normal life right there.

He comes back with a plastic bag the size of my head.

I'm staring like a vat-grown virgin seeing their first lover starkers. Burning hell. I almost got myself killed for a fourth of that on Irithessa. This will set me up for a year, if I'm careful. Right on time, my arms and legs burn, like they're coming alive at last.

It's almost like that dumb story I asked John Starfire about, where the old Jorians could stick a corpse with a soulsword and bring it back to life, not just tear it up. Except the only thing I've been stuck with is the sight of drugs.

He presses it into my hand. "For Death." I let out a deep, heavy breath that I didn't even realize I was holding. I shove one of my shaking hands behind my back, so he won't see it. "I'll take that letter of credit in exchange. Perhaps I'll find a fool who thinks it's worth something."

"Yeah," I slur, my tongue even more frozen than usual. So many pinks. So much music, here in my hand.

"Come on now," the priest says. The NecroWasp rises from the table, shuffles along grunting, next to me, out the door, along the length of the courtyard, to the muddy path back to the port, where Rashiya must be wondering if I'm coming back.

I look up at the NecroWasp's beautifully hideous face. "Loyal."

"As long as you are loyal to Death."

That's one way to deal with Terracor, if it comes to that. No soulsword's going to stop something already dead. I keep this thing close, and when I need to break with the officer I don't trust, I'll have one guaranteed backup.

It almost sounds good. Like a plan.

Until I thumb the pinks in the bag, and I feel my head go light, and my whole body tingles. Yeah, this is me, ready to up-end the Resistance and save those kids and keep that asshole Terracor in line. This is me, who can't even go without a hit for a day.

11

Jaqi

I TURN ON BILL's shower. He warned me that I would get exactly a minute. He's lucky enough to have collected a cache of comet water before he went dark, or I would be subject to a cleaning-field that would mean a mild burn all over. Instead, real water, a genuine cocktail of hydrogen and oxygen pulled from actual ice (and a bit of recycled piss; can't be choosy).

It rushes out nearly as cold as space. I do the little dance I learned over the years here. Face, armpits, sides, butt, crotch, one leg up, other leg. My hair slaps against my back and I run my soapy hands over it, hoping to make at least a little progress.

The water is just starting to warm up, and I'm almost done shivering, when it shuts off.

Short, but the best damn thing in the galaxy. Nothing beats a shower after months on-ship. It would be a bath, but we reckoned the kids needed the basin more. I reach out and grab a towel, one of the few Bill won't use for grease spills or general repairs, and dry myself off.

I wipe away the last remnants of Swiney Niney dirt. The last of the grease and anti-oxitate from Palthaz's ship. The last of the sweat and stink of the crickets' ship.

I step out of the shower and sigh.

"Done?"

Z is standing there, also in his starkers. And he's got those tattoos *everywhere.* Black patterns, some of them looking like book-letters, going across every inch of his evil white skin, up around the two curved horns that stick out of his forehead.

Not bad, though. The guy's got muscles like molded steel. Scars every foot or so on his arms, chest, neck, and legs, marring the tattoos. I always liked a few scars. A lover can't be too pretty.

"All yours," I say.

He crouches and goes into the shower. He's holding those armored synth-scale trousers. Suppose he's going to bring them in the shower; not many chances otherwise to clean them.

From inside, he says, "At home we scrub with sand. I cannot understand this much water."

"Sand en't exactly a comfort after a long day in the grease," I say.

"It is wasteful."

You know, if he weren't such a joy-killer, I think I would ask if I could join him in there. Get a little bit of the old slack. It's been a mighty long time, long enough that I can't afford to be picky, and by the look of him, everything would work, if you get me.

Just my luck to be traveling with a nice big slab, everything right except his brain.

He speaks up, over the rush of water. "Do you believe in the bluebloods' God?"

"That's a hell of a question to ask in your starkers."

"I am curious. You have paid back the debt to their brother a few times over, yet you still seem reluctant to abandon them.

I wonder if this is a conviction of faith."

"En't that," I say, and go quiet for a minute. "I don't know what I believe, scab. I done this cuz I reckon it's right."

"That is a form of belief."

En't anything, I think, but now's not a time to argue, as I'm drying my bits. "What about you? You into this God—or gosh or what you call—and the Starfire and whatnot?"

He sounds annoyed. Well, actually, that en't any change from normal. "The Starfire is not something you choose to believe in or not. It simply is."

"Scuse me, mister preacher."

"The Starfire is the fuel that burns in pure space. The original Jorians could touch it, and did great miracles with it, and made the nodes so that the other races could spread across the stars. Humans grafted their idea of a God onto the Starfire, but it is an older, greater force."

"That don't sound too different from this God."

"No sentient has seen or touched God. You touch the Starfire each time you take a ship into pure space."

"Hold on, scab. I en't having no religious vision when I find a node."

"You think not," Z says, and finishes the shower, stepping out to towel off every inch of his tattoos. "But that is what it is. Crosses are imperfect copies of the old Jorians, but the old DNA breeds true in some of you. That is why the Empire was afraid of crosses breeding, of crosses who made art. They feared the resurgence of the old powers."

Now he's truly talking crazing. I find nodes just cuz I can, not because of some thing burns in pure space.

I ignore him and get dressed. Bill's kept some of my old clothes. They're a bit too small. I didn't think I had any growth

104 • *Spencer Ellsworth*

left in me, but I guess I do. Going by what Bill reckoned, I must be near eighteen, Imperial reckoning. Short life, for all the living I've done. Can't think of a lot of eighteen-year-olds who shot one of the Vanguard in the face and lived. Yay?

I head over to where the kids are, across the common area. Bill's got four bedrooms and a bathroom set off the common room to the left, and then a massive hangar full of all the matter he's smuggling to the right. The hangar is five times as big as the living space, which is why it was so much fun to play in as a kid—as long as it was pressurized. Even a rascal little girl knows to stay away once the atmos is gone.

Bill's sitting with the kids, playing his guitar. I recognize this song he's mumbling his way through. "I knew a girl, she rode the nodes, she rode the . . . furmble mumble mumble . . ." Bill gives up and starts whistling the tune. Bill en't never learned anything but dirty scab songs.

"Do you know 'God of the Stars, God of the Earth'?" Kalia asks him.

"En't this a sight!" I say to Bill.

He looks up at me and grumbles, "Doing the best I can."

"Jaqi!" Kalia jumps up. Her and Toq run and hug me, and clearly have no intention of letting go.

"You two smell good."

"Bill made us do a bath." Kalia's face twists. "I told him I wasn't going to bathe with Toq, but he said we had to. I haven't bathed with Toq since we were really little."

"It's okay," Toq said. "I like it."

"You almost *peed* in the water."

"But I didn't. I got out in time."

I've learned, by this point, not to say things like *What kind of catch can afford to bathe separately?* I guess that's what happens planetside. Kalia can just go ahead talking about life like we're all eating off the same banquet table.

"I wanted you to come. I'm going to give Toq a reading lesson. You should sit with us."

"Not now, kids," Bill says, as a couple of lights go on in his monitoring screen, and I can hear that apprehension. "I need you to come see the Suits."

The kids tremble, and I put my arms around them, for all that I'm relieved he just saved me from a reading lesson. "It's okay," I say. "The Suits can hack that black box. The code that Quinn knew. Then we'll figure out where your dad wanted you to go."

"I . . ." Toq is trying hard not to cry again. I hug him close against me. He's mighty warm, and shaking. "I don't like it. It was Quinn's. I don't want anyone else to touch it."

"I know, but with Quinn gone, we're going to have to hack it. Quinn would want us to know what's on there, honey." I stroke Toq's hair. "Go on and cry. It just hurts when you keep it in."

Bill is patient, thank the stars. He waits while the kids get up, all slow and trembling. I don't think they like talking about that fancy black box. Reminds them too much of Quinn. I can't blame them. He was a good kid. Stupid, but good. And going by his talk, he knew more about this whole situation than these kids did. Maybe he even knew how this nonsense was supposed to work, all about heading out of known space.

We cross the living space of the station. Kalia is clutching the black thing, and Bill's running lights shine off the inscribed letters and fancy curls on it. The door to the hangar takes up one of the walls, and as it slides open, some of our warm air gets sucked out. The air's always colder and thinner in the hangar, when Bill can even afford to pump atmos through there.

Bill's normally got crates stacked as high as those Swiney Niney buildings in here, but this morning, there's only a few crates scattered about the floor, Bill's ships and ours parked at the other end of the floor, a mess of steel and busted circuits and gear matter for the Suits to play with, and Bill's ship-sized water tanks. Haven't seen the place look so empty before.

One of the Suits scuttles across the floor.

This one en't too bad, as far as the shivers go. It's big, but it looks a bit like a man. Well, a man and a bug, and a bit of machine, and . . . never mind, it's a shiver all the way. It's got a man's torso, and a man-sized head, with a visored helmet. Man's arms, though they've got various spidery extensions. You can see a bit of a man's face through that visor, with actual human eyes, though they don't blink, staring just straight ahead at us for so long they make my own eyes start to hurt.

Instead of arms below the torso, he's got long girders, run with wire, ending in flat pads for walking. Seven of them, making him look half man, half white spider. He's got all sorts of spanners and welders and hack-arms built into the arms above the pads. Easy to work from a lot of different angles.

The Suit sounds human when it says, "Do you have the data?" Flat and boring voice, even though it's twitching like it's eager to get the data, and that voice could have come from any typical scab, not one hacked to bits and mixed up with junk scraped out of all the galaxy's dumps.

Kalia holds up the black box. The Suit raises its arm/leg/whatever, and the pad that served as a foot shifts, rotates, and folds up inside the girders that make up the lower part of the leg. A bulb, covered in running lights, rotates back out, and a couple of clamps extend from the bulb.

"Give it over," I say to Kalia. The Suit's clamps take it from my hand, and little sensors emerge from those clamps. The sensors are like live wires; small cords, dancing across the surface of the black box, looking it over for ports. They find a couple of spots I didn't even realize were there—must be hidden ports in those fancy letters—and then the Suit's circuits start humming, and the little clamps squeeze. A series of numbers flashes across the Suit's visor.

"This might take a bit, for it to run the hacks," Bill says, but as soon as he finishes, the Suit's flatly human voice speaks.

"Too tightly protected. Take it to the mainframe." It drops the box.

I grab the box before it falls. "Hey! Be careful with that!" Kalia hollers.

"Mainframe," I say. "Where's the mainframe?"

The Suit doesn't answer for a moment, processing something. And then it says, "You are not permitted."

I'm about to slap the thing, metal or no, and Bill grabs my arm. "It's okay, Jaqi." He pulls me back, whispers to me. "I know where a mainframe is."

"How the—" On the scale of secrets, the location of Suit mainframes is up there with the color of the emperor's underwear.

"It's . . . it's not a nice place. We'll be safe, though."

"Safe? What if the Suits want to hack you up for spare bits?"

He half smiles. "It's the Engineer's place, and he always honors a bargain."

"I en't never heard of no Engineer."

"Never you mind." Who's this Engineer? Some intermediary with the Suits? I'm about to ask, but Bill clenches his jaw, purses his lips. Familiar, that. Means he's got a thought, and not sure whether to say it.

"What?"

"You en't coming, are you?"

"I . . ." I mean to say *I don't know.* Bill's always said *I don't know en't worth much but the "no."*

Z approaches us from the back, and, as usual, breaks up the mood. "I have heard what you will say. For enough money, I will go with you to this mainframe."

"Oh, that's good, en't it? Cuz if there's one thing I have, it's a catch," Bill says.

"Your water is worth money," Z says. "Your tech. Your connections." He crosses his arms. "You need me. You will find money."

"All right. All right." Bill's staring past us. Into the main room of his place, at the comfortable chairs, the wooden table. The rack of guns. That guitar, the neck all worn down from years of playing. His place, he carved out of rock his own self. "I got a couple good ships, besides that heap you brought in."

"Hey, that heap's running real nice, thanks to us," I say.

"Hope so, because it's all yours," he says to me. "Wish I could give you more."

"I en't . . ." I want to say *I en't going to leave you.* But it sticks in my craw. Normal life. It sounds too good. I look at the kids, real long. They'll be running forever, while I finally get to stop running.

That's when the Suit, with even worse timing than Z, looks at us and says in that flat, almost-human-but-for-the-deadness tone, "I am sorry to report that a ship has come through the node, without codes. We have been unable to stop it. It appears to be a Belthuin assault-class. We will arm defenses."

Vanguard.

12

Araskar

I STAND AS CLOSE as I can to the NecroWasp in the bay of the ship. It sure is ugly, and not in some casual way, like a black eye, like that ecosphere was. This is ugly high art. This is the core of ugly, around which all other ugly orbits. The way those segmented eyes pop out of the head, a little too far, straining all the veins around the lids, the way those mandibles stick unexpectedly out of the human parts of the head, leaving a kind of crusty torn skin around the edges, the way that head doesn't quite sit right on that neck and it has to really pop the muscles to keep that head up . . . damn, it's so ugly it's beautiful.

I might be a little stoned.

"So," I say. "You're all mine."

It doesn't say anything, but I get the distinct impression it is listening.

"We've got a little mission. Heh. Really, really little." Strains of music twine around my head. Little notes soar over my head and come to rest in front of me, vibrating deeply along the lines of the universe, tickling my skin. The music is avoiding this monstrosity, though, the notes swooping and ducking away from his ugly mandibles. "We're chasing a couple of kids, and if you and I are separated, you need to watch those kids. They are not for Death, you understand?" It cocks its head, which causes a vein to stand out in bright relief under the skin. "The kids. Not for Death. If you must kill to protect them, you kill." I poke its chest and immediately regret it. It feels like poking a rotten mushroom. "Don't let anyone get the kids with a soulsword, with a shard. I promise you I will send plenty of other folks to our Necrotic Lord."

It'd be nice if this thing nods. I decide that its cocked head is close enough.

It's a fun curiosity. Half my scabs have already come down to get a look at my new pet. Terracor hasn't said anything, which means he's not bothering, or I'm just confusing him. Whatever the case, I float along nicely to my room.

I just took a couple of pinks. The day of withdrawal was good for me. I was up to five or six pinks at a time before. I have more control now, ai?

Which is how, when I see Rashiya waiting in my room, I just smile. "Come for the view?"

"Get in here," she says. "I'm sick of this." She grabs me by the shirt. "Let's just pretend, for an hour, that I don't still think you're a bastard."

She doesn't say much after that, though she makes plenty of noise. Once we're lying there exhausted, and my body is enjoying a much nicer comedown than it's ever had, she clutches my chest, rakes her nails across the skin. "Don't be stupid anymore, Araskar."

No comment on that. "Let's go back to Irithessa," I say. It'd be nice if it was dark in here. The nonoptional lights are starting to hurt my eyes. "Drop this Vanguard thing. Go into public service."

She laughs. "What are you going to be?"

"Well, before I had to get pieces of my hands replaced," I say, "I was going to be a musician."

"A cross, playing music?"

"That's the whole point, isn't it?" I say. "Show the galaxy that we're sentient. No music, no art, and any cultural context needed was on the data dump when you were first sparked up." I hold up my hands. Only two synthskin fingers, truly, and they don't give me the trouble my leg does. Holding those chords always killed my hand, though.

"You know, when my father came online," she says, "crosses were still being encouraged to read. There was a whole program. You read a certain amount of literature, wrote a few papers, got a small certificate of schooling." She leans into me.

"Ha," I say. "There was a sea change on the Empire's part. I went from vat to violence in a week."

"Well, you were still made high quality." She squeezes my high-quality parts.

Barathuin and I read our first book when we were trying to find our names. It was a collection of stories from the First Empire, and just about every cross raided it for good names. I can still hear his voice. *Barathuin. A warrior-king of the First Joria Epoch, who slew the thunder-beast.* And me. *Araskar. Some random soldier, and it doesn't say anything else about him. I like the sound of it, though.*

He laughed at me. *You do know what "scar" means, pretty boy?*

"Your children will have that chance now," she is saying. She lifts her head up. "Once this is all over."

There's not much to say to that. We've never discussed children, given what we've seen of the universe. I finally say, "Consolidation won't ever end." And there's that old Marine in my head again. *Not till the whole galaxy goes dark.*

She gets up, throws on that thin, circuit-laced bodysuit that gives her a personal protection field. "So, you'll be in charge of aerial support on this mission. I'm taking your division for the burrowing pod."

Hang on. I had to have heard that wrong. "What?"

"You heard me."

"Hell no! I'm not even a pilot!"

"You trained with the Moths in boot," she says. "Bolt up, sit back, feel the instincts, and let the Moth do the work. I don't want you to engage directly. We need someone like you calling orders."

"I won't— I should be with you!"

"I'm sorry, Araskar. Terracor asked for recommendations, and I recommended that you stay back for this one. Coordinate the flyers. Make sure that nothing gets in or out."

I stand up. "I'm not taking this. I'm not on the pinks." My tongue slurs on the lie, but I ignore it.

"I believe you," she says.

"Then let me go in with my slugs."

I think for a moment she's going to change her mind. Then she says, "Araskar, we don't trust you. Manage this. Then we'll see what you can do on future missions."

"Damn it, I don't deserve this."

She cocks an eyebrow. "We're just taking down a few minor defenses and snatching a few kids. You really all that worried about your slugs?"

"I'm always worried." I grab her shoulder, tighten my grip harder than I should. "Promise me you won't hurt those kids. We can't hurt children."

I can't tell if she's lying. She sure can't tell when I'm lying. They say the original Jorians could reach into each other's minds, read them like a navigator reads the nodes, in the invisible currents of the Starfire that drove them.

All I've got are her eyes, steady and green as two cold stars.

"We've got five minutes to report, and fifteen minutes to

node-drop," she says. "We'll take your pet. That thing is so ugly a few shards might improve it."

A simple change of orders, and everything goes to shit. I hate to even think it, but I did this to myself.

Jaqi

"How far out are they?"

"The node is jammed," the Suit says, ignoring me. "We are attempting to open."

"I can get us through the node," I say. "Just hold them off while we get on-ship."

"The Suits can only hold them off for a bit," Bill says. "I've got two mounted guns on the rings, and they've only got a half load of shards in them. I've got . . . nothing else, except the gunner ship, and except what's in there." He points toward the rack of guns hanging in his main room.

"Me and Z will have to hold them off. You much of a shot, Z?" I ask him.

"I can shoot," he says.

"You're going to have to. Get out," I say to Bill, to Kalia, to Toq. "Get out the second the Suits can open the node." I try to smile for the kids. "Don't worry, Z. I'll hold your hand."

"I'll pray, Jaqi," Kalia says.

Well, I reckon that might work as well as anything else I'll do.

Bill's Keil-118 gunner sits at the far end of the hangar. Good ship, from back before Keil started churning out substandard stuff. All rivets and steel chopped out of good earth and melted down, no synthesized bits. Bill runs back into my room. Z runs for the gunner ship. "Keep up!"

I don't complain, for once. I run with him.

The gunner ship is not much bigger than Z. Cockpit, two engines directly to the side, auxiliary wings, folded in now, for flying in atmos, and a gun pod slung underneath, with two fat, gleaming barrels, all fused steel. A thick tank of shards sits under the engines. The tank is the only weak spot—shielded as it is, encased in a thick layer of metal, one good shot would still blow the little ship to pieces.

I heard once that the galaxy was all projectile weapons, before some genius figured out how to shard an atom—shave electrons off unthunium and tear folks to pieces much more efficiently. Must have been a nicer place, when you just got a piece of metal lodged in your meat, rather than shards tearing flesh and melting bone before they burn themselves out.

Why am I thinking about this now?

They should have made crosses not to think about stupid things before battle.

I grab the ladder. Z takes a long look at the pod. "I will not fit in there," he says. He puts one of them massive hands on my shoulder, like he's supposed to be comforting. "I saw you shoot. You be the gunner."

"Me? I'm a pilot. En't no sniper."

"You have shot Vanguard. I have not."

"If you're trying to be funny, Z," I say, "this is a bad, bad—" Bill's hangar starts to open over us, and the atmos screams right out. Z's up the ladder and in the cockpit quick as death. I jump into the pod. "—time."

Z was right about not fitting. I'm crammed in there, my knees touching my chin. I grab two levers just in time to twist crazily as we go up, ship shaking from the force of the atmos pushing at us. The ship rises as air leaks out of the hangar. Z's got the thrusters on full, shooting us up hard, too fast, and then he fires the stabilizing thrusters, trying to get his bearings, spinning us around in vacuum. He's a terrible pilot—or maybe that's my stomach doing flips.

Bill's asteroid falls away below us. Surrounded by clear plasticene, I'm suspended in the dark, with only this monstrous gun, silent except for the hum of the engines above me. To my right one of the rings rises, a white arc through space, and as Z swings the ship around, I see the running lights of the Vanguard ship, a blot against the Dark Zone's black sky. Tiny specks of light are spilling from the Vanguard's cruiser. Gun barrels are blazing away from Bill's stabilizing rings, and shardfire cuts a wide red path across space, lighting it up like we've just ignited a star for this place.

My throat is aching, and it en't just because my knees are pressed against it. Sweat is rolling down my back, for all that it's cold in here. I don't want to die like this. I don't even remember what that burning trick was I used to shoot the Vanguard before.

Z must hear my panting up in the cockpit. He says, "If we die, we will die in blood and honor."

I en't read none, but I figure that's the worst inspirational speech in history.

Araskar

I don't know what to say to Helthizor. We stand in the hangar, and all the slugs I kept alive on Keil's moon mill around me like dumb puppies, even though Terracor's bellowing to get into the burrowing pod. They all look at me. Some disappointed. Some surprised. Most seem like they're waiting for an order.

"I don't like this," Helthizor says.

I can't afford to agree. "It's nothing, slugs. Just . . ." I look at Terracor. He's, for once, taking point on this mission. "Just use your sense. This is a simple snatch-and-grab. We've been through too much to be afraid of a snatch-and-grab." I lean into Helthizor. "No soulswords, no killing," I whisper. "Not for children. That's an order."

"Yes, sir," he says. He leans in closer. "But, sir, they're humans."

"What?"

"They're just humans," says Helthizor. "We've all heard, sir. We all know what has to be done. No one said consolidation would be pretty."

What is this? "Someone besides me give you an order? About humans?"

His face tightens up. "No, sir, no orders; I guess I was listening where I shouldn't have been."

"Yeah, you were, soldier." I struggle for a moment—do I ask Helthizor about this thing, and acknowledge that my gossipy slugs know more than I do, or do I wait to confront Terracor?

Terracor bellows something, which decides things for me. "Go. Snatch and grab and we'll talk later."

Helthizor shrugs, and says, "Got it."

I salute, and we all roar, "Stamp your boots and open your sheath!"

I run to the end of the hangar, for the Moths, unfurling from their white plasticene cocoons. The six-man squad of flyers has put in extra hours for this, though every soldier here trained with a Moth.

Moths evolved on a wild world, one no one paid attention to because of the way it lost atmos after terraforming failed. Wormy sentients lived underground, and grew a bone-hard, spiny-winged carapace that recycled carbon dioxide into oxygen and kept them nice and warm, if a bit sticky. They could vent carbon dioxide in jets, which allowed them to fly for weeks beyond orbit and harvest water from their icy moons. Perfect natural space-ships, and it was John Starfire who figured out that crosses could fly them with a bit of training. Those worms were more than will-ing to give us used carapaces, for enough coin.

My Moth's enclosure is wide open, the carapace gleaming pink inside, the hard, brown outside studded with spikes. A gun has been mounted in place of its original feeding tube.

"Hello, sir," says one of the other pilots. "I'm Jevathor. Nice to have the Secondblade flying with us."

More like the Lastblade. "Whatever you do, stay on the pod. We can't let them hit our boarders. I've got the field—just listen."

He salutes. Polite kid, considering they don't need my ad-vice. Still, I've got orders, even if they're shit orders, and I'd better act like the big boss according to those orders. I take a moment to slash the soulsword across the meat of my arm.

Blood lights the blade with white fire.

I climb into the Moth, sticky and warm, like—never mind what it's like. The carapace closes, and I thrust the flaming soulsword up, into a slot made for the fin-brain of the original inhabitant. With that, a channel through my soulsword ex-tends my awareness to the carapace, a part of me now.

I can see outside myself, in a blurry, bisected way; my vision stretches in a vast bug-eyed circle. I see the hangar as we leave. I see the unnaturally dark space ahead of me. I see the wide rings that make up this establishment, and I see the gun barrels the boss of this complex has installed. The guns spit bright red shards against the darkness. The asteroid blinks with light, far below us, and a tiny gunner ship jets up from its hangar.

"Formation fall, in twos, to the guns," I say, and the other Moths pick it up, into their soulswords and their thoughts. We fall through vacuum, our own shard-fire answering the guns. Shards dance across the blackness. Shards explode against wire and metal and plasticene, break the rings into glowing fragments. One of my slugs catches a big gun under its carriage, at the supply pod, and it bursts in a massive flare of red shards, tearing the ring apart, sending fragments of metal and rock and plasticene through the void.

Then a shard rips a Moth, turns it to meat. We all feel the scream, vibrating through the soulswords, as the poor slug inside dies.

Those mounted guns aren't automated—something with a brain is targeting us. In this sector of space, it'll be the machine men.

"Back off, back off," I say, over protests. Stabilizing jets of carbon fire, the Moths rising as though they really are riding currents of air. "Those are Suits behind those guns. They're predicting us. No more formations."

From the heart of the complex below, the little gunner ship rises toward us, lurching back and forth, trying to stabilize. Through my circular field of vision, I see our burrowing pod, stuffed with my slugs, drop from the belly of our cruiser. There's Terracor and Rashiya inside, and my whole squad, falling toward the asteroid. Ready to board, and I'm up here.

I dart for the gunner ship, and fire, protecting my slugs.

13

Jaqi

UP WE GO.

"What the hell are those?"

Z doesn't have an answer. Big brown bugs? The Vanguard has some funny allies. They circle the rings of Bill's asteroid, trying to take out the shard-cannons that Bill's Suits installed. Their wings are spread out, hard and veiny and traced with black and brown designs that kind of remind me of Z's skin, truth. They've got shard-fire spilling out of their mouths, and one of them is coming for us. Its shard-fire traces a line across our left side. We're hit, and the ship shakes, spins evil before Z gets it under control. "Fire!" he yells.

I fire crazily, a wide burst of shards at this insect. No good. I distract whatever-it-is—but it en't real shooting.

"Shoot like you mean it!" Z snarls. "Shoot like you did before!"

"How did I shoot before?"

"Shoot!"

Oh, that helps. Damn. I grip the handle and let off a spurt of shards, and they go flying well off into the darkness. The brown thing spins, fires.

"Shoot!"

"Dodge!"

Z does an admirable job, I must admit, piloting, but he en't got the touch I do. I'd better make some shots count. Too bad I en't much of a shot.

How'd I do it before? I was as panicked as a girl can get. I suppose I'm close now.

It was like a node. Like finding a node, the way I reach out, find that one little slit the old Jorians opened to pure space. Invisible to everything except the right code transmitted on the wormhole engine's frequency, or the eyes of a cross with the talent. I can grab a node and I can pull us in, and before . . .

Before, on Swiney Niney, I grabbed that gray bitch's brain. I grabbed her like a node, and I shot, and the shard-fire just soared right to her. And I can tell you something, now that the bugs are close. There's Vanguard in those brown bug-ships, and if I reach out I can do the same.

Araskar

Oh, hell.

Why am I suddenly crazing? I can hear the music. Not some smooth fine background noise—it's blasting in my ears, a screaming, dissonant roar this time, a wave about to break—

I take a hit.

My Moth's wing breaks away, alight with the red glow of the shards, pieces flying bright through the darkness. The skin on my good leg shreds and freezes, exposed to vacuum for a second before the carapace closes over it protectively. I fly up from the force of the blast, away from the asteroid, and I fire the Moth's stabilizing jets. But I've lost half the jets, so that sends me into a spin.

I've never had the music come sober. Or had it come with this burning pain. I fight the fall, spin the Moth. I am fighting a little of the asteroid's gravity now, and the shards bring their own burst of hot gases, throwing off my flight.

The gunner ship gets above me. Whoever's on that thing, they think I'm out of this fight.

Above me, Rashiya's burrowing pod falls closer.

The gunner ship is moving into the perfect position to meet it.

I fly right at the gunner ship, steering with my sword. I twist my fingers, about ready to fire, to take out the gunner ship—

Everything goes numb, like before. I can't feel my fingers. I can't feel my arms. My stupid fake tongue is limp in my mouth. I can't control the Moth.

No!

Jaqi

I got him! One of those bug wings breaks apart, sheds fiery pieces as it goes spinning into the vacuum.

"Yes, good," Z says. "Fire again. Blood and honor!"

"Tomatoes!" I try to lock on to one of the other insects. The calm is gone, in that rush of actually hitting something. I reach for the node, the sense of connection, but I don't have enough time. The rest of the insects are flying interference, farther above the asteroid, trying to take out the cannons, and now trying to take out the three Suits scuttling up and down the rings. At least the Suits are giving us reinforcement.

One of them damn bugs connects, its shards blowing through Bill's ring, breaking apart the cannon and tearing one of the Suits into three pieces, metal and flesh separating and spinning off into the black. Bits of metal rain down on us, pulled by the asteroid's gravity—Z jerks the ship back and forth, trying to dodge them, but we still take a nasty hit, and we're listing, spinning on our side, and I see—a pod, coming from above, one of them pods meant to board a place—

"Z!" I yell. "Take that pod!"

He pushes the ship, up and up, to meet the burrowing pod that is falling rapidly toward Bill's. That's the one, soon to be vomiting Vanguard into the halls of my home. That's the one I've got to hit.

Without stopping to concentrate, I let off a bright burst of shards at it, and miss by a good mile. Z is yelling something, no doubt something unhelpful about honorable death and maybe some blood. I try to concentrate. Node, it's a node, I'm focusing, feeling the space between us, closing the space . . .

Not as easy as it was with just one of them. There are a good fifty Jorian crosses on that pod, and they're throwing off my sense. I can't grab onto any of them. I fire, and fire again, and miss, and miss again, and I reach and reach—

Our ship spins, gone crazing. My head jerks to the side, knocks so hard against the window that my vision blurs. "What—"

I open my eyes and there's a bug on the windshield. The insect-ship I just shot has crashed into us, its hard and horned brown body wrapped around the glass, blocking the gun. Its own gun head is lurching, back and forth, trying to get a place to shoot from the gun glued into the insect's mouth.

I can see, though I can't say how, the fella inside the bug. Big scar across his chin. His eyes are wide and he's coated in sweat.

Z is turning and diving, turning and diving, trying to shed the thing, but it's got spikes in the clear plasticene around me, holding tight, and I'm trying to pull the trigger, but it's shoved up against the barrel, forcing the gun back. If I fire, the gun will jam, and we'll all blow to hell.

"Do something!" Z roars. "Get out and scrape it off if you have to!"

That en't going to happen. But maybe—

He's a young guy, with enough scars on his face for a lifetime. Old eyes. Right now, his body's shaking. He's afraid.

It's all connections, I'm thinking. All like the nodes, these connections between Jorians. Like the Starfire, what they talk about in old times.

So I *push*.

I shove him away like closing a node.

And the bug-thing tears away from the ship, goes spinning out into space, and I have a clear view, at last. Bug fighters dart for me, trying to cover for their burrowing pod. One of Bill's Suits drifts in the black now, firing at the bugs. They fire back. Metal Suit limbs go spinning off into space.

The burrowing pod is within a few meters of Bill's. Grapples launch from the front, hook into the rock of Bill's asteroid, pull it closer. All fifty Vanguard in there are going to drop in, on top of the kids and Bill, and I zero in—

I fire. I fire a beautiful big volley, the shards spinning across space, bright yellow and red and trailing clouds like blood in water.

My shards catch the burrowing pod. They blast it open,

shred metal, molten pieces splitting and careening through space. Vanguard bodies fly out. The fire tears their bastard faces and their bastard arms and their kid-killing swords and I fire again, and again, the shards shearing their bodies down, ice-chunks of blood and limbs and heads making a pattern across the vacuum. I kill as many as I can hit.

"Blood and honor!"

That was *me* saying it.

Araskar

I can't move.

I can see the cross in the pod. Starfire knows how. She's tiny, dark-skinned, black eyes reflecting the red light of my shard-glow. She's looking right into me. Like she can see everything, and I know she only wants me to be meat, and I can't move!

The music is overwhelming me. Tears leak from my eyes at the beauty of it.

It's her. She's the music.

She pushes me away.

I go spinning off into darkness, like a piece of frozen debris. The notes of the music are a frenzy, a storm of slicing metal, ripping through my veins, and my whole numb, frozen body just won't move, just locks right up, not even a twitch of my fingers—like a damn baby, like meat in the vat, like *nothing*, and I can do nothing—

Nothing but watch, as she kills my slugs.

Her shards connect with the pod. The metal turns white,

then bursts open. Bodies fly out, targets like animals flushed from their hole. The shards keep coming. My slugs sail out, and her shard-fire cuts them into pieces, into lumps of meat and bone and freezing blood across the emptiness, just like my friends, the same faces, the same blood, the same way they are just meat, turning to nothing but meat.

My face is too numb to scream.

The music rises to one final crescendo, soaring strings, hammering drums, roaring walls of notes.

Jaqi

Z is shouting something in another language, in triumph. I shout, "Contact Bill! Tell him to get out now! *Now!*"

I'm still shooting—firing up, at another insect ship swooping down at me. "Z, did I get gray girl? Is she in space?"

"I don't know," Z roars.

That pod made contact before I blew it. If gray girl hung on—if a few of them made it in, when it was burrowing—then Bill and the kids are dead.

If not, I could bug out. Bill might be safe, now. I could take Z and I right into a node, right now, far away from this craziness. As long as Bill and the kids left safely—

Shard-fire hits us, and there is a loud *boom,* we shake and the air hisses with atmos escaping. We're in trouble.

Z pilots the ship down, toward Bill's hangar. Too fast. We're going to hit hard, possibly ignite our shard-tank. Hangar doors are open, but nothing's changed—the bare floor, the Suits'

126 • *Spencer Ellsworth*

pile of junk, the water tanks, Palthaz's ship where I left it parked—and then I can't think any more, because we hit.

We scream across the ground, metal on metal. We crash into the Suits' pile of junk, send it flying.

Under the scream of metal twisting, I can feel the roar of the shard-tank at the base of our ship. If it breaks, we're gone. The ship will be gone, the whole hangar gone, the whole asteroid up in fire. I grip the bars below the triggers, hang on, knuckles white—

The ship hits the wall of the hangar, throws me against my chair so hard that my breath collapses in my chest. After a moment, I open my eyes. We're still here.

The hangar doors screech closed overhead. Closed? But Bill! The kids! They should be bugging out! Atmos hisses through the space around us, Bill's precious air filling the hanger.

I unbuckle slowly, painfully. Crosses are built to take punishment. Nothing broken, right? Built for punishment. Built to crash ships and fight Vanguard and . . . I struggle up, force my hands to grasp the ladder to the cockpit. I pull myself up through the tiny passageway.

Quinn, you brave bastard. Jaqi, you dumb scab. Z, you . . . He's alive, but he's unconscious, and he's taking up the whole damn cockpit. I reach over him, my hands scrambling across the controls. Dark take us, it's cold in here, so cold my fingers feel like they're collapsing. I punch the keys and open the cockpit.

I mutter, "Up, Z. You're not dead in blood and honor yet. Up!" I slap his face. Nearly breaks my hand.

His head rolls around, revealing eyes that are rolling in their sockets. "Up!"

His head comes up, groggy. "I—"

"Blood and honor!"

"Blood and—"

Bill's head appears over the cockpit. "Jaqi, oh my Dark-gone girl. Come on."

"Bill? Why en't you gone?"

"Node en't open! I been sitting, waiting, but those bugs got all my Suits." He looks over at the hangar door. "Good shooting, girl. Come on, let's get you and this lug out, you can jump me through the node, then you can go about your—"

The hangar doors, to Bill's living quarters, to my home, open. It's dark beyond, fire flaring in the limited atmos, smoke billowing, but I see that white-fire glow of two soulswords. Aw hell. I missed some.

-14-

Jaqi

I DON'T THINK. I raise my gun and shoot.

And I miss.

Gray girl runs out of the smoke, same color, carrying her sword, flashing white against the darkness. She's got her head unwrapped now, orange hair springing every which way. Behind her comes a bearded fellow in body armor. His soulsword is up and at the ready too. Blood drips off his hand, and when it hits the ground, it sizzles white.

And behind them—that damn NecroWasp!

"Oh, come on!" I groan at whatever fates are listening.

Bill springs down from where he was. Beard-face is heading for the ship, where the kids will be. Gray girl and the stinking Necro-Shit are heading for us. I shoot again. My hand is shaking. The shards go wide and leave smoking trails across the metal of the hangar floor. The three of them dodge and weave, but they're in no danger of being hit.

If I shoot wild any more, I could punch holes in this place and send us into vacuum.

When Bill hits the ground, he fires, evil precise. Gray girl raises her sword, catches the shards, and they go flying.

He keeps firing and she keeps catching shards—until he's out.

Bill decides to act the damn fool and rush her. "I en't never harmed you!" Bill yells as he runs at her. "I ran guns for your Resistance for ten years, you back-stabbing swine."

"Run . . ." I say, but as beat as I am, it comes out as a groan.

"You're not worth my time," gray girl says. She grabs a pistol from her hip, shoots. The shard-fire tears Bill in half.

"Bill!"

I shoot her before she can react. Wish the shard-fire would tear her in half, but she's still got her protection trick—it just knocks her flat. I keep firing. I unload the whole clip on her, and it spins her body across the floor like a blackball gone downcourt but it doesn't touch her skin.

"Shit." The gun's empty. Quality antique piece; holds only a fingerful of shards. I try to jump out of the cockpit. I just crash to the ground, in front of old NecroWasp, who still stinks like the whole galaxy took a shit together. "Nice to see you," I mutter.

The NecroWasp reaches for me with its clawed arm. Its stinger gleams, venom dripping from the tip. It hisses something with that mandible mouth—the usual *Death!*

"Rrrrrraaaaaaaa!" Z leaps from the cockpit onto the Wasp's head. With them big fingers, he reaches behind its big black eyeball and rips the eyeball out, splattering himself with NecroWasp juice. "Go! I will die here! The ship! Go!"

I get up. Gray girl is still lying on the ground.

Beard-face is walking into the ship, where the kids are. I run, but I en't got a weapon—my gun is empty. Gray girl's soulsword lies there in front of me. I grab it.

I en't ever held a sword in my life.

Got in a knife fight once, and got myself good and cut by the Kurgul on the other end of my knife. I seen what the Jorians do, though, when they fight, once on the news screen.

Maybe it'll work for any cross, even a scab like me. It's all I got.

I slash my arm, carefully, not too deep. Everything hurts so much already I hardly feel it.

My blood leaps up the blade. Just jumps right up and turns white, and then the black steel turns white too, with fire.

And I feel something, almost like the soulsword's my own private node. We're connected, like this soulsword is a piece of me, ready to burn through the world.

Damn.

I run up the ramp into Palthaz's ship, where the kids are. I duck under the metal braces, past the locked cargo bays, into the common area.

The common area is lit by the white of red-armor's soulsword, a good three times brighter than mine. Everything is scattered. Bill's guitar and all the kids' clothes are on the floor. A case of clothes is chopped to pieces. He is standing over Toq. Poor kid lies on the ground, staring up. Kalia is against the wall, not moving. Dead? No, she's trying to move, arms flopping. Bastard probably got a nerve cluster, or hit her on the head.

Beard doesn't speak. He's all business, raising that sword to kill a couple of children.

Toq bites his leg. Beard snarls and kicks out, raises his sword—

I run him through from behind.

I en't never stabbed anyone before. Good thing I'm evil juiced, cuz I ram that sword in, screeching past bone, harder than I ever hammered in a nail or a rivet. The way that flesh gives and resists at once—it en't a good feeling.

The soulsword turns space-cold in my hand. It's like a pillar, connecting my arm to his insides, and I can feel him die.

His memories come flooding into me. This man's killed more people than the primaria virus. Dead, dead, dead Kurguls and other crosses and traitors and humans, and I see him all the way back to the vats, I see battle after battle until he dreamed about blood and shard-fire, until he didn't care. *The whole galaxy is just meat.* That's the thought drives this man.

I see he's got a fella, someone he loves, back at home. People are funny. He goes out killing kids and then he goes back to his fella and they sit and hold hands and read.

He's rushing into me, his memories, his loves, his whole life, up my arm and into my heart, out my veins, into my brain.

Then he dies. Like that. Falls to the ground.

After a moment, I fall down too.

"Jaqi!" Toq is sitting on me, hitting my head. "Please! Wake up!"

I look up. There, down the ramp, the NecroWasp is coming for us, a long trail of goo coming out of its eye socket. It stops at the ramp, and does something I wouldn't have thought. It speaks, a low throaty grumble thick with mucus.

"He wants me to spare you." It starts up the ramp, its stinger protruding, bright with the gleam of poison. "My new owner does not understand. Death is mercy."

I don't think I can move.

Z jumps up behind it, all blood and snarls. He reaches around its belly and grabs the thing's stinger, and with a roar like a beast gone rabid, he rips the stinger off and jams it into the Necro-Stink's head. For a second, I figure it en't done anything—but no, even this thing can't take a spike in the brain. It topples and slides off the ramp.

Z, all over bloody, crawls up the ramp.

I look up into that tattooed face. His veins stand out even against his tattoos, thick rivers of black. There's a little welt on his chest. "Thought you were going to die. In blood and honor."

"There's no honor in being killed by something that's already dead."

"It stung you," Kalia says, pointing to the welt on his chest. The little spot's all swollen and black.

"I have been poisoned before," Z rasps. "Go!"

I slump into the cockpit. Don't know whether Bill got the coordinates programmed in for his big secret mainframe. Looking out the cockpit, I see that gray girl is gone. Damn. I wanted to shoot her. I hit the hangar controls, and above us the doors open—

A hail of shards cuts apart the hangar. The bugs, and the Vanguard ship, and everything up there rains down hell on us. "Jaqi!" Z shouts. "Jump! Jump!"

I reach out and grab the node, and I jump us blind.

It's cold.

It's dark.

Where the burning hell are we?

I can see the kids, and Z, but hardly, as if by some kind of pale, sick light, kind of thing that shines from the rotten vegetation in Swiney Niney at night. They look all washed out. The light is faint, white, a little blue. Feels almost like the memory of a light, something I create out of my own mind.

Kalia's eyes flicker open. She looks at me. The blood makes

a line down the side of her face. "Where— What happened?"

"Vanguard came close enough to kiss is what happened." I don't see anything out the viewscreen. Nothing but blackness. Nothing but—

"Jaqi?" Toq says. "Jaqi, I think I hear something."

"I don't hear anything," Z says.

"I hear someone." Toq looks up at me. He looks a bit too much like his brother. "I hear someone talking."

I reckon I hear something too, now he says it. I hold a hand up. Z's got his usual scowl on, aimed toward the viewscreen. The viewscreen that is completely dark, with not a star to be seen.

I hear something, all right. I hear little whispers, and they turn my skin to ice.

We know you.

We watched you. We watched you, when you tore their bodies. We watched you, when you cut him, he who is dead.

"Do you hear it?" Toq's voice is marred by his pitiful little-kid trembling, trying to form words when it's killing him. "Do you?"

I look out the viewscreen. It's dark. Total, black darkness, the kind makes you feel like you've gone blind. And yet, out there, if you look long enough, you can see traces of that ghost-light. Little, small blips of white and blue, almost enough to give a shape to the darkness.

My skin was cold, but now I feel weirdly calm. I shouldn't, with a voice from nowhere saying it's going to eat me. But I feel, at last, like I don't need to think. I don't need to think on my feet and fight my way through this. I can just rest in the darkness, in the voice.

I stare into the darkness, and I start to see it all.

Those little, faint rushes of light illuminate a darkness strung together. Hints, edges, vague shapes of a web, thick strings running together, knotting, fibers and cables of absolute blackness the size of planetary systems.

Tens of millions of knots and strings and patterns, into the infinite distance. Like the collected cobwebs of a million star-sized spiders.

"Do you hear them?" Toq is going to cry.

I reach out absentmindedly, stroke his hair. "We're fine." We are. I am so calm.

We are going to eat you.

"We are in the Dark Zone!" Z says. He seizes me by the shoulder. "Jump us!"

"But . . ." It sounds so nice. Just to lie back, and let the spiders crawl over me, drag me into the darkness. There won't be anything in that darkness, except a hungry maw. I won't have to shoot Vanguard, or swing a soulsword, or anything. I'll just let them eat me, slowly.

"We will not die here!" Z says. But his normal growly roaring voice is just a small thing next to that whispering warmth. "This is not where we die, Jaqi!"

We are coming to eat you.

The flashes of sick-light increase around us. It's so dark it's hard to tell, but I could almost say that something is moving along the cords of those webs. Something vaster than a star, and alive. Many somethings. The cords tremble.

"It's okay," I say. "It's okay. We'll like it." I won't remember Quinn dying. I won't remember Bill dying. I won't remember . . .

I won't remember my mother, either.

Strange thought. I haven't thought about my mater in some

time. That memory comes, my first memory, of her sprinkling salt on a tomato slice. The tomato is big and red and glistening under our flickering lights. Her voice is singing a field-worker's song. Bend, pull. Bend, pull. I remember her hand as she gives the tomato to me, the soft, sweet, sharp taste.

Like sunlight . . .

I don't want to forget my mother. Odd thought, that. As nice as this warmth is, as nice as it sounds to go into the dark and be consumed, I don't want to forget the dirt caking her hands, the way her fingerprints were creased with black and the edges of her fingers were cracked from picking crops. I don't want to forget the way she slid the slice of tomato into my mouth.

I don't want to forget Quinn. He thought I was worth saving, and I can't just let his brother and sister get et . . . Don't want to forget Bill.

No.

"Shit!" I'm not warm anymore. I'm cold. Freezing, like ice is eating me up an inch at a time. The kind voices turn to hisses, to loud screams in my ears, scream after scream after scream slicing into me.

"Where are those coordinates?"

"Right in front of you, idiot!" Z says.

He's right. They're flashing on a readout, clear as day, but in this darkness, it makes it burning hard even to focus. Everything's getting darker, all around us. The Shir's screams are high and cutting; they rip through my muscle and bone and open my heart. *He promised you to us!*

I en't never seen coordinates for this node before. It don't matter. I reach out, find the node we must have jumped through. Even in the Dark Zone the nodes are here; it opens for me and sucks us in—

They're fighting it. I can hear their screams, and the screams have a kind of force, like a wind wrenching at you, pulling you off your feet.

Outside the viewscreen, I think I can see a face, in that sick half-light, an enormous, old face with a hundred eyes and wide broken rings of mandibles and a million spars of teeth, the size of a planet. *We will not let you go.*

"Burning hell you won't!" I grab the node, and I force the jump, sling us into pure space.

The Shir's cry of agony follows us into the white flash of pure space. As our ship bends and pitches through speeds much faster than light, their screams echo and echo and echo.

15

Araskar

I FLOAT AWAY FROM the asteroid, away from the heat of the shard-fire. The music is gone. It's been replaced by the eyes. There's a few hundred of them now, but only fifteen faces; they all share the same fifteen faces. They're all staring at me out of the darkness. Every last dead one of them. *Are you mad at me for living, or are you telling me I'm just about dead?* No answer. Impolite bastards.

The Moth around me is growing cold. It's been hours since this one left its cocoon chamber, and they degenerate if they don't go back in.

Through the Moth's circle of vision I can see the asteroid, floating up above me, still glowing with shard-fire. I can see the white of the rings, broken, pieces spinning in space. There are bodies up there, or pieces of bodies.

They were all just kids. Hell, I've been five years out of the vat. Were I someone's true-born cub, I'd barely be reading.

What did they think they were doing? When the Empire built the first crosses, built us out of the Jorian DNA in their labs and the DNA of humans, trying to make the right combination for the perfect soldier—why did they think that they could construct us only to kill, and yet they made us able to feel?

We fought this war, this Resistance, because we did not just want to be killing machines. And here we are. We failed. We overthrew the Empire, but we are nasty bastards, and have to find something else to kill.

It's colder.

And something stirs. Far, far out, light-years away, something springs into my head. It's her. The girl with the music. Not gone after all. Something was keeping her from my senses, but now she's there, stronger, drawing me. I could find her, if I wanted to.

I push the thought through my soulsword. *Back.* Return to the ship. If there's any strength left, go. *Back.*

My hands move, thank Starfire. The Moth trembles. And then two of its thrusters fire, propel me up. Didn't even know they were working.

I need to find her. I need to end this.

"He wants to see you."

My Moth is lying frozen and useless across the hangar floor, a brown wreck, its ragged edges rapidly shedding skin, turning to papery shreds that scatter across the hangar with each blast of new atmos. I can't walk. Two of the survivors—there's only about ten of us—have hoisted me up, put my arms around their necks, and slid me along the floor. Rashiya's eyes are deep-set, in hollow pits. That gray protective suit she wears has been torn, revealing lines of fine wire and circuitry.

"Who?" Half frozen, my tongue's even more useless. I stand in the middle of our ship's hangar, conspicuously empty now without the burrowing pod and most of the Moths. "Terracor?"

"Terracor's dead." She's barely standing. Shard-fire has burned away her left ear, turned the circuits and running lights that were part of her face into melted slag. "That little cross bitch got him."

"I felt . . ." I felt the girl, full of music.

Rashiya waits. I don't know what to say. "You felt what?" she asks.

"I felt nothing," I say finally. "Thought I was dead."

She looks at my leg. I can tell what she's thinking. It's not the kind of wound that should have taken a Moth out. I stand up and stare at her. Perhaps she can tell, from the way I am, from my weariness, that something else is wrong.

I think about the way my whole body went numb, in the face of the music. Numb, just like I knew it was going to one day, with all those pinks.

I'm just about ready to tell Rashiya to throw me back out the airlock when she says, "Dad. Dad wants to see you."

And that's how, a few hours after I choke when it counts the most, I am sitting before a grainy viewscreen consulting with our fearless leader.

John Starfire looks older. He's still got the salt-and-pepper hair and beard. His eyes still have a kindness that he didn't pass on to his daughter. His jaw quivers and he tries for a smile, and fails. "Araskar." The pure-space relay blurs his words a bit.

I don't say a word.

"You failed," he says.

Strange to say, but that's almost comforting. I wait for what he's going to say. Whatever it is, it'll be soothing, in its way. *You're relieved of command. You can get high and die.* If it weren't for the girl with the music, it would sound good.

"Araskar, if you were anyone else, I'd throw you into a prison."

I nod.

"You're different, and I need you, even if you failed. You have something that other crosses don't." He stretches out his hand, from where it's been clasping his sword. "Araskar, I can feel the Starfire. I don't often tell people this, but I can. I can feel the power driving the universe, and when I need it, it aids me. Do you feel it?"

I don't answer. I just sit there. This is of a piece with everything—our leader's crazing.

"Like a flood, Araskar. Like currents twisting together in a torrent."

"Yes, sir."

"Like music, whole symphonies rising in the distance."

I perk up, blink. "Music?"

"Have you felt it?"

"I . . ." *I was blazed as a supernova at the time.* That, and *then it came from a girl who shot me.*

"I believe, Araskar, that we are not crosses, but are the first generation of the new Jorians. Do you believe that?"

I just nod.

The Chosen One keeps talking. "We will grow stronger and stronger, until we can make our own nodes, until we can return to the old galaxy and find Earth that was lost. Do you know what a memory crypt is?" His hand is out of the frame. I'd be willing to bet all of lost Earth that it's twitching on that sword handle. "The old Jorians used to seal up their greatest knowledge in memory crypts. They would remove the knowledge they had sealed up, remove it from the minds of the entire galaxy. It was knowledge that they wanted to make available only to Jorians, and once the old Jorians died, the bluebloods couldn't access the information. Only a true Jorian can access a memory crypt. Listen." His face is cold now, cold and hard and serious. "When we took Irithessa, the first thing I looked for, in those ancient vaults, miles deep in the crust of the planet, was the vault of memory crypts. I've been reading about them since I was a child. I found them. I was able to read them, Araskar. Do you know what that means?" He moves closer to the screen, and his voice takes on that odd, robotic quality. "That means that we aren't just crosses. Like I've always said, we are Jorians, as much as the ancients."

I nod.

There's an edge, a hint of something—a fear?—in his voice. "One of the memory crypts was gone. It could only have been a human who took it. If it had been one of the Resistance—one of our own—we all would have known." He leans in. "Do you understand now? I sent you because I know you are like me. I knew it as soon as I saw you—you will sense things. Your thoughts will go farther. Your heart will go farther. Rashiya told me about your problems with drugs, Araskar, told me about how you've been trying to kill what's inside you. Stop."

I force myself to meet his eyes. "Sir, I'm no different than any other cross."

John Starfire lapses into that grin, but it just seems fake now. "You're a hero." And then the grin falls. "Crosses are mostly blind to the power of their ancestors—made simply to breed tough. You are not. You are like me, and, as I've told you before, that means you have to act like a hero whether or not you know you are one."

I think of the girl. The girl in that gunner ship, with the mu-

142 • Spencer Ellsworth

sic. I'm no new kind of Jorian. I'm no different than any other cross. But if there was one of the ancient Jorians reborn, I'd bet on her.

When I leave, I go straight to the bridge. I look at the star map for the systems around the Dark Zone, in the wildest of the wild worlds, and after a long time, after a long time asking myself whether I can truly do this, I point toward a system where I know that girl is.

I give the coordinates to our navigator.

16

Jaqi

WHEN I OPEN MY eyes again, the viewscreen has the most blessed view I've ever seen. A sun, white and bright in the distance. Visible planet and moon in the distance of the viewscreen. A veil of comets falls through space, so slowly you can't tell it's moving, shedding clouds of ice that obscure the view of the planet. A world hangs in the darkness, night-side facing us. Even from here I can see flickers of artificial light in that world's atmos. Glimmering patterns of life. Its moon shines, big and close, beyond the horizon of planet.

"It's beautiful," I whisper.

"Indeed," Z says. For once he doesn't sound like a burning lunatic.

"Oh my gosh. Oh my gosh." Kalia is huddled up in the corner. I crawl across the floor, scraping my knees on the grate—everything still hurts—and reach out for her.

"Come here, honey."

"Don't touch me!" She pushes me away. "You were going to let those things—those *Shir*—eat us!"

"They were convincing."

"I can't do this anymore!" Kalia screams. "I want to go home!" She stands up, runs to the common area. "Quinn's dead! My brother's dead, because of you! You should have saved him! You're going to get us all killed! I just keep praying and praying and you—we all need to repent!" She storms out.

Now that is some top-quality crazing. I want to run after her, but I'm also so exhausted I just want to die.

Maybe she en't crazing. It's true. I should have saved her brother. I should have saved Bill.

Toq grabs my leg. "You can hold me."

"Okay." I let him crawl up into my arms, cradle him like a baby. He nestles his head into my collarbone and drools a little bit, the warm spit collecting in the hollow of my shoulder.

"I was really scared," he says.

"Me too," I say.

"But I didn't pee this time."

I start to laugh. I can't help it. There's just something funny about peeing your pants. Toq laughs with me. That makes it worse. We keep laughing, nervous, for a good three or four minutes. We keep laughing until Toq coughs and hocks a large ball of spit right into my shoulder. I still don't move him.

Z is staring after Kalia, toward the back of the ship. I lean my head back into the captain's chair. "You okay?"

He coughs. "I will live," he mutters. He's shaking, moving one hand across the welt the NecroWasp's stinger left on his chest. "It only grazed me. Just—water. I need water." He takes a few halting steps to the locker, opens it to reveal the tank of good clear comet water Bill stored here. He presses the button and the water tank hisses open, and he tilts it and sucks down water for a good minute.

"You sure you'll live," I say.

"My people know poison," he says, his voice sounding a little better. "The Empire has been trying to poison us for centuries." He sinks down next to us. "Our blood fights."

Yeah, I think his blood is losing that battle. "We need to get you help."

"Just let me drink the water," he says. "Enough water, and I will be fine." He points at the comet, a haze in the viewscreen. "I will bring us alongside that comet over the next few hours, and we will have enough water."

After a while, Toq coughs, a dry one this time. "My throat hurts," he says.

"More water?"

Z hands us the tank. It's mighty awkward, but I get it tilted up and Toq sucks down some of the sweet, sweet water. None of this reclaimed piss.

"I'm scared," Toq says, and coughs on the water. "I'm scared all the time."

I think about saying *Me too,* but I don't want to jitter the little guy. "We'll be safe here. I got us to . . . wherever we are. We're evil safe."

"I don't want to leave the ship," he says. "Let's stay here." And then, easy as you please, he looks up at me and says, "Is God real?"

Oh, hell. "Nobody talks to crosses about these things, kid. Crosses have to believe in surviving. We en't got the luxury of believing in other things."

"If we die, I want to be with Quinn, like they say in church." He nuzzles against my shoulder. I keep expecting him to say something else, but I guess that's all.

"I want you to be, too."

I am, suddenly, sleepier than I've ever been in my life. No matter how tough they make crosses, I'm not tough enough for this. So Toq and I crawl into Palthaz's tiny bunks, where my head brushes the bunk ahead of me, and we wrap arms around each other, and we go dark.

Z wakes me up a few hours later. He looks worse. That white skin is turning green under the tattoos.

"Z, you look like shit! You shouldn't have let me sleep!"

"We're being hailed."

"By who?"

"The planet."

I stumble out of bed. "The Suit mainframe? This that Engineer Bill talked about?"

"Those were the coordinates Bill punched in." Z sounds worried about something. "I don't believe he told us everything."

"Who's hailing us? Suits?"

"Kurguls."

"Kurguls?" I stop in my process of stumbling through the hallway. "You didn't let them see the kids, did you?"

"I'm not an idiot, Jaqi," he snaps.

"Excuse me, Mister Takes-On-NecroWasp-for-Fun, but you en't exactly making a reputation." I sit in Palthaz's chair. Z collapses into the co-captain's chair.

A Kurgul comes on-screen. He's got a wide-brimmed hat, shading his eyes. Leaves enough room to see the scar bisecting his lips, and the way one of his tentacles has been truncated about a foot down. Taken a few hits, this guy has. Maybe we'll get lucky? Maybe this is the galaxy's only decent nest . . .

"You the Engineer?" I ask, when he hesitates.

"I'm Swez. I represent the Mataka nest's interests on the planet of Trace."

I mute us. "Burning Dark and shit in space!"

"Matakas," Z groans. "Wish us blood and honor, ancestors."

"That too," I say. "Also, burning Dark and shit in space."

Matakas have the same space-black soul as other Kurguls, but they en't got the light touch—a Mataka's "gentle persuasion" is another sentient's nuking from orbit. (That en't a phrase. The Matakas truly nuked the Tsukani nest from orbit. Tsukanis were evil good customers, too.)

I switch the link on. "This is . . . Jaqi. Come out on behalf of Bill; you know, dark-spot Bill."

"I know him," Swez says, in that Kurgul rasp that I hate so much. "Where is he?"

"He en't here," I say. Have to fight the old block in the throat there. Bill's gone. Just like Quinn, sold his life to protect something he don't even know. I'll have a good cry over him, soon enough, soon as I can stand it. "Sent me with something for the mainframe."

Swez shows a bit of his sharp teeth. "You best turn around, 'less you got some serious matter to offer," Swez says. "Nothing goes to the Suits without going through the Mataka."

Z cuts in. "There are children here. From Keil. Perhaps you have heard of them?"

"Z, what the hell are you doing?"

I finally see Swez's eyes, because the little red dots go wide under that hat. "You're the ones who have the whole galaxy alight, are you?"

"They are being pursued," Z says, his voice rasping, "because they have a certain item. A small black box, from the First Empire. We have attempted to hack it, but we cannot. A Suit mainframe could do so."

What is he thinking? Didn't he just tell me he wouldn't say anything about the kids? I whack him on the back. He sways a bit, but stays in place.

"We don't want no trouble with Vanguard," Swez says. "We

keep the moon, and the Suits keep the planet."

"You will not have any trouble," Z says. "Rather, the reverse. This information is too valuable just to let the Vanguard take, my friend. This information will be worth the entire fortune of your family. Imagine, the Matakas, in the favor of the new rulers of the galaxy."

"Or on the ends of their soulswords."

"Do you never take risks?" Z asks.

"Only with folks they're going to kill anyway," I mutter.

But Swez surprises me. Suppose it's because he's a Mataka after all. "We will allow you to approach. You will not be able to leave, though, without passing on the information."

"Thank you," Z says, and cuts the transmission. "Time to go."

"What the Dark were you thinking?" I ask him. "You just did exactly what you said you wouldn't do!"

"I made a calculated risk," Z says. "I could have tried to hide our nature from this Swez, and he would have shot us from the sky. Or I could tell him the truth, and trust his greed. I believe in Kurgul greed."

"And if the Vanguard offer more? Or stick Swez with a soulsword? You could have made up a lie they would like as much as the truth, a lie that didn't put the kids in danger!"

"Imagine that I tell them the children are not here, but the box is," Z says. "They would simply kill us and take the box."

"Nothing's stopping them now. They could come aboard and kill you and me and take the kids."

"They could try. I think the Kurguls fear me." He coughs. "They could blast a hole in our ship, let our atmos escape, and then come after the box in the wreckage. But they cannot do that if we have the children, since they must know the Vanguard want the children's memories. They could try and board us, but they know I will kill many of them."

"In your state?"

"I am fine," he half snarls, but I notice his knees are pressing against each other, locked up. "They could come after the children once we reach the surface, but we will be surrounded by Suits there."

"And you couldn't have thought of some lie that wasn't as good? Like—like we had the sword of John Starfire, uh, sewn into our skin or some matter like that?"

Z says, in all seriousness, "I am not a good liar."

"Well, I . . ." I was about to say that I am, but I reckon that right now, having just faced down the Vanguard and the devil himself, I wouldn't have come up with a thing. My brain's been all wrung out. "I . . . I guess I'm sorry. Maybe." That en't much. I add, "I gotta confess, Z, you're smarter than I thought when I first saw you standing there in a fighting pit, all ready to die."

"I'm glad I didn't die there," Z rasps. "I did not realize that NecroWasp was already dead. There is no honor for me in being killed by something already dead."

"You mentioned that," I say.

He sinks into the seat, lets out a long, wheezing breath. "Jaqi."

"Ai?"

"Don't let me fall asleep." He grips the lever.

"I'm with you, Z."

We've nearly come alongside the comet. The planet is much closer now, filling half the screen.

"What'd he call this place?"

"Trace."

"As in not a." Good name for a place we've gone to disappear.

He's going pale.

"I'm getting you water."

"No," he gasps. "No, stay here. Keep me talking."

"What's your story, scab? How'd you end up out here?"

"What do you know about the Zarra?" he asks.

"Some of you got tattoos and some of you don't," I say.

"There is that. Some members of my race joined the Empire. Others did not. Those of us who didn't had land—sparse, difficult land, but land. Until the Empire wanted it for their mines."

"Sitting on a cache of shards, were you?"

"Sitting on the land where my grandfather died," Z says, and I can't tell if he's still sounding like death, or sounding a bit like a regular old sad fellow. "On the water we drank for a thousand generations, and the deer we hunted, and the trees we cut and the desert where we learned to survive from our fathers and their fathers. Now, you are right, it's all unthunium mines. We are crowded into our little parcel of allotted land, and paid in increments. My father sits alone and angry in his little hut, and drinks. My mother left him and left our land parcel. She had her tattoos removed."

"Those tattoos mean something?"

"They are the names of my grandfathers, and grandmothers. They make up my entire name. Zaragathora is but a piece of that. It's . . . also not really how it's pronounced." He lets out a long, rattling breath. "Zaragathora was . . . a dramatic choice." He closes his eyes.

"Hey, wait! Can I still call you Z?"

"Yes." He opens his eyes again.

We're closing with the trail of the comet. I can see beautiful crystals of ice, streaming over us.

"Activate the comet still," I say. "That red thing up there. You pull out, then down."

He raises his arm, groaning. We slow, enter the trail of ice, enough to collect water. It cuts out precious time, but you can never get enough good water out in the wild worlds.

It takes a steady hand to fly in the comet's trail, and Z has to monitor the still, and then we have to break off properly and close the last of the route in with the planet. Tricky business, takes time, but it keeps him busy, and moving. I can't help noticing that welt looks awful. It's leaking a little bit of black liquid, oozing slowly down over his ribs and his thick slabs of stomach muscle.

"By the Dark," I say, as we close with the planet. I reckon there's a few storm clouds to deal with, but that still don't stop me from seeing that a good continent of that planet below is solid light. Lights stretch over most of the night-side of the planet. "So that's a Suit mainframe."

As we get closer, the metal appears, thick in orbit. Suits are everywhere. Every shape—snaky ones a mile long, ships the size of Imperial dreadnoughts that move a million little crane arms—and spidery ones that give me a new shiver, given some of them resemble the devil. Every combination of organic and mechanical you could imagine, all jumbled up, moving among scrap, gathering their things together.

Z speaks up. "I left home," he says, "because there was no chance to earn honor there. Many of my people have done the same, gone to the wild worlds. I wanted, originally, to return and restore our honor. Now, I . . ." He looks out on the screen. "I just want to live a life worth living."

"Well, Z, if we live through this, I reckon it'll be right worth it." I clutch his clammy hand. "So live through this."

———————

Araskar

The shrine sits alone in the middle of the meditation room. Not much of a shrine. The bodies we could recover have been cremated, and their ashes have been placed in an open urn, so wide it takes ten paces to walk around.

What was my slugs is now powdery ash, heaped in high dunes and sickly white under the running lights of the ship. It has a subtle stink, like old bones boiled for soup. There's Helthizor, and Salleka, and every face I screamed at in training. There are the backs I shoved up the Bastard, running that hill over and over, the skins I saved on Keil—all in that ash.

Cremation is supposed to be a way to honor them, since recoverable cross bodies, under the Empire, went back into the vats for spares. No cell was wasted when there was meat to be recycled and remade, the raw material for synthskin and synth-flesh and whole new crosses with the same faces. Now we honor them, let the crosses be burned like real sentient beings. But damn it, I wanted to see my slugs' bodies. Even torn apart, even meat going into a vat, I would rather look in their faces.

I kneel down and I draw the short sword at my belt. The great soulsword takes another's memories; the small soulsword exists only to take your own soul.

The short soulsword shimmers faintly in the running lights;

the currents of black steel, hardened into a short, curved blade, subtly variegated like a jewel.

"In token of my lost honor," I say.

I let the blade linger when I cut my arm, let it groan and burn. From the blade, grasping fingers move through my nerves, bursts of climbing pain that reach into my brain.

———

Barathuin breaks the bottle against the edge of the table. Beer sprays everywhere, along with broken glass, flying off into the darkness of the makeshift tavern in this tent.

Real glass. Fancy beer, that. He shouts and raises his soulsword in the air. "Starfire!"

"Oh, for burning Dark's sake, you're going to get us shot," I say.

"Nothing can kill me," Barathuin says. He can't help his voice from slurring and slipping. His face is threaded with bruises, and his arms, and he stinks, not just of beer, but of blood and sweat from the fighting pit. "Nobody can kill me today, Araskar. I have won the . . ." He squints at his trophy. It might have been a Kurgul's tentacle, if the tentacle were made of shredded and repurposed aluminum foil. "I won the soulsword trophy."

"That's supposed to be a soulsword?"

"What's it look like to you?"

"I'd tell you, but you're too young." He roars with laughter at that one. I stand up. There's plenty of girls, and fellas—Barathuin likes both—waiting for a chance to talk to the winner, and who knows, one of them might turn out to be good for him.

I go and sit at a table. I've drunk just enough to feel warm. Tonight, it doesn't matter that we held an illegal tournament, which even the Resistance would frown on, or that we're holed up in a compound under a biosphere on an empty rock that's a mile too wide to be a comet, that we have defied a very strong order to bring the booze to the line untouched. Tonight, my friends and I are together, and getting the drunkest we will ever get, before we hit the campaign next week. Next week we will jump into burrowing pods and hit the Imperial Navy ships broadside, and take on the trained crosses of the Empire with nothing but our guts and our wits.

Hell. Those thoughts require several more drinks.

"You." She grabs my arm. I come around to snap my hand on her wrist—reflexes—but she stops that too. Red-haired girl. The one who creamed me in the pit a few hours earlier, the one who gave Barathuin the fight of his life.

"Hey," I say. "We were looking for you. Hope you're not sore." I grin in a way that Barathuin has mastered, that half-ac-cusation, half-playing grin. "I still am."

"Shut up and drink." She sits down, across from me, and grabs a half-empty bottle from another table, clinks it against mine. "For the Resistance, and your stupid friend."

"For the Resistance, amen."

She drinks hard. After a couple of beers, she orders shots. After a couple of shots, she pulls me close to her, gags me with her pickled breath, and heaves, "I'm still sober." I could almost believe it, except that I can hardly believe my own senses, so who knows if that's what she's really saying? "I hate this. I can never get drunk."

It usually takes quite a bit of booze to get us drunk; she might be an espionage model, meant to never get there.

"What's your story? You must be top of the line. I haven't seen your like before."

"I'm home grown. Real parents."

"No shit? I never met one of you real ones before. So that's a face no one else's got?"

"This is just mine," she says, spinning a hand around her cheeks. I laugh and she waves her hand. "En't all it's cracked up to be," she says. "It's not like coming from a vat; my sisters are scared I'm putting all of them in danger, and my dad, well . . . don't ask me about that bastard."

"Seems like you bred true," I say. "You beat me like you were gold-grade Marine stock."

"Yeah, you weren't quite the challenge I thought you'd be back there, slab."

"What?" I sputter into my beer.

"I can tell when a cross is holding back." She takes another shot. "You're one of those who needs to see the devil in front of you before you can swing a sword."

"Walk out! I know I hammered you good."

"You know what, slab? I reckon I am tingling a little bit." She looks up at me. "Feel like hammering me some more?"

What's she mean? Another fight? A rematch or . . . oh. Oh.

When I don't answer, she adds, "You're a fully working model, right, slab? Do I need to conduct an investigation?"

"Uh, fully working." Vat-grown eunuchs just don't make good soldiers. Thank the Starfire for little things.

"Ever used it?"

I don't respond to that. I haven't seen her at officers' mess anywhere. She's just rank and file. "I'm sure I outrank you."

"Some comfort that'll be when you die a virgin."

Well. She's got me right, much as I hate to admit it. "Then

you're under orders to keep your mouth shut."

"That's what makes a good night, in my experience," she says.

"Why me?" I say as we get up. "Why no other slabs in this room?"

"You walking me off?" Her face turns to a pout.

"Not at all. Let's go. Just wondering why me."

"You're special. Shut and follow me, special boy."

"I'm special? How's that?"

"I don't know," she says. "Fine, you're not special. I just need a warm body."

You're like the war that way, I almost say. But it seems I have finally learned to shut up, and that is indeed the key to a very good night.

17

Araskar

I CUT THE MEMORY. The memory of that night when I first met Rashiya, when the tournament we had played was over, when Barathuin was victorious and my batch was still alive. We sat at the table and drank and laughed and she straight up asked me back to her bunk.

The small blade lights up with white fire, with the energy of the memory. I hold it out, so the light of the soulsword's fire shimmers across the dunes of ash.

"I have given up a piece of my soul for my honor," I say softly. "I will take it back only when I've truly honored you."

That old story still gets me. I first read it among those legends of the original Jorians in that book where Barathuin and I found our names. Some fellow, whose name I don't care to remember, had a soulsword that could actually take a soul. Not just a psychic resonator, made in a factory, matched to a cross made in the same factory, poured in a mixture of true metal and synthsteel.

No, this one had a magic sword, and when he went into battle, he tore the souls of his enemies and pulled them into his blade. Unlike putting meat back in the vats, it was real life, it was the glory of the Starfire and the currents of the universe that folk talk about.

And when his friends fell, he used the souls of his enemies like fuel, to bring his friends back alive. Not a joke. In the story, he sticks his dead friends with the sword, and up they pop, using the souls of his enemies as fuel to bring his friends back, same as putting meat back into the vats.

They fought an army of demons, granted, and then flew on a dragon to a moon, so it was a shit story.

A soulsword good for something besides tearing through guts and ripping out memories. Wouldn't that be nice?

But that's not what a weapon, be it a piece of metal or a piece of vat-made flesh, is for.

The blade blurs in my eyes, the gleaming white fire on black steel. I could put it in my chest, right now. I could make the ultimate move of the dishonored, and let myself fall forward into their bodies, finally join them.

I sheathe the small soulsword.

Then I withdraw the pinks from my shirt. I show them to the pile of ash. "These were more important to me than you," I say. "No more."

When I try to put the pinks out the airlock, my hand spasms on them, worse than John Starfire's hand twitched on his sword hilt. I clutch at them and I think of the music and I think of forgetting the war and I think about Rashiya and what lies in store and I think of the girl in that gunner ship and my slugs, and my friends, their faces over and over, and damn it, damn it, I want to forget. I want it to all be gone.

My hand twitches and twists, going numb. The synthskin in my fingers feels the most alive of the uncontrollable hand. I let go, my fake fingers first, and somehow, after an eternity, my real fingers let go.

I watch as the airlock opens and the pinks are sucked out.

The bag rips and they scatter in the vacuum, bright for a second in the ship's running lights, like tiny stars.

———————

Jaqi

I speak the message, and it flashes across the screen, not that I can read it. "Here to see the Engineer. From Bill's." I figure this Engineer's got to be some fella works with the Suits.

The Suits' reaction is instantaneous. One of those dead, flat voices rings out. "You bring the data."

"Uh, yeah," I mutter. A string of Suits drifts across our viewscreen, a half-dozen bundles of metal arms and tubing and bulbous heads.

"Come. We shall program your coordinates." The numbers flash across the screen, bright green, lighting up Z's face as they go.

Down we go, toward the mainframe.

I forget to switch off the itchy artificial gravity before we hit atmos, which means there's that moment of strange brain squishing when gravity clashes before I throw the switch. "Sorry!" Good old regular gravity, tossing us around like fish in a tank, little heavier than I'm used to. I never learned the percentages, but I know good gravity when I feel it. I figure the Suits might have modified planetary mass just for their humanoid visitors. At least, the ones they en't going to slice up.

They en't going to slice us up. I don't think.

Something else hits me, a realization. "Whoa," I say, as the thought hits me. "Z... this is my first time planetside since . . ." I look over and his eyes are closed. I punch his arm. "Z! A planet! I en't never been to one since I was five!"

His eyes open, glazed over. I punch him again. "My first real planet, Z!"

"You have . . ." He finds his voice. "Never breathed real air?"

"All ecospheres and stations," I say. "We were on farms, when I was real little, but most of my memory, it's been these places." A real planet, not an ecosphere. Hell, even a Suit planet is a real rock circling the sun. First time. It en't no Irithessa, but still . . . I'm flying in real atmos. As the bluebloods would say, the way God intended it.

"What is wrong with the air?" Toq says.

A yellow haze spins below us, too fast to be a regular storm. Fingers of lightning run through the yellow cloud. Beyond it, the morning sun is hitting a vast black landscape of triangles and squares and lights glowing with lights, red and green and white and blue. More yellow haze looms on the horizon, clouds of it mixing with the smoggy purple-white of regular clouds.

"That, my friend, is a nano-Suit swarm." Creepy, I have to say. I've heard of them. They roam the galaxy, spun off from their "parents," who tap into quantum storage and create microscopic cells capable of flying up to whole ships and dissembling them. "I hope they were warned about us."

"What would happen otherwise?"

"Otherwise . . . they swarm this ship, pick it to pieces. Or worse, turn it into a Suit, just waiting for organic bits. Welcome to Suit Central. Try not to puke."

"I saw a Shir," Kalia says. "I don't think that Suits scare me anymore."

"It does my calloused self good to hear that, it does," I say. I guess I can't trouble her for naming the devil, given that we looked it in the eye. "Toq, you scared?"

"I don't know," he says. "It doesn't do much good to get scared out here, I think. Everything is scary. You have to get used to it."

En't that one of the wiser things I've heard in a time?

We descend. Around us towers, black and spiny, stretch up toward the sky. Biggest towers you'll ever see; I don't think even them famous pyramids of Irithessa could dwarf these. Their tops are lost in that yellow haze of nano-things. Flyers zip everywhere, carrying things from one tower to the other. Below the towers stretches a tangle of city; all steel and wires and lights, a living machine that covers the continent.

"They're moving!" Toq says. "The towers!"

Sure enough, two of the big towers have a set of little legs coming out of the bottom, walking them around. Their thousands of lights glimmer on and off as they slowly trudge through the metal and Suits thick as flies.

If you look closer at them towers (and I evil hope the kids don't), you could see the sacs. The Suits have their own kinds of vats, growing organics that are best suited to splicing into their parts. You could see full-grown men and women, blank eyes staring from the gel they're kept in while they feed from a tube and shit in another tube.

"All the junk of the galaxy. Bill traded them whatever he could find," I say, "even if it was just old pieces of plate. They go through everything for information. Probably could bring down the galaxy if they wanted to."

"Why don't they?" Kalia asks.

"They don't think like that. They're hungry for scrap and data. New material to process. New components to break down into fuel. New organics to splice. If they replaced the

Empire, no one would want to sell them information."

The voice that booms over the link is another almost-human thing, save it's too flat, without tone. "You have data."

"Most precious data in the wild worlds," I say. "If you can crack it."

"We will send you coordinates for our data center." Sure enough, the green screen lights up with the numbers. Easy enough. Just punch the numbers, and we go into the guts of the Suit mainframe.

We sweep lower. A yellow cloud spits from a round smokestack, and I can't avoid the damn thing. I swoop right through it. I swear, for all that they're microscopic, I can hear the little nano-Suits pinging off the hull.

"Ah!" This time the cry comes from Z, of all people. "Watch out!"

"Can't help it, Z," I say. "They won't hurt us as long as we're holding the data over their heads."

"It . . . it seems . . ." He doesn't finish that sentence.

I look over and see Z is licking his lips. "You okay, there?"

Z don't answer.

We zoom in closer, between buildings. They're all moving. Even the buildings that aren't alive, Suits themselves, are crawling with other Suits. Some of them even move on two legs and two arms, though most of them have decked themselves out with a couple of hundred legs. It's like a nest of ants. Like when you turn a log over, and all sorts of crawlies run everywhere, like . . .

"Ew! Ah!" I jump in my seat.

"What was that?" Z asks.

"Nothing. Just . . ." The Suit we just passed looked about as much like a centipede as anything can.

"Are you frightened of something?" Z says. "Think of what you've seen."

"It don't make no sense," I say, "but a girl gets to be afraid of a bug now and then. En't you got something you're afraid of?"

"Dying of old age," Z says, his voice a dry whisper.

"Oh hell, Z. Don't joke about that."

Kalia whispers something. "What's that?" I say. "You talking to me?"

"I was praying," she says. Sounds about right, in this mess of metal moving around us like a bunch of bugs. And though I don't ask, since it's none of mine, she says her prayer. "Our Father, who art in Heaven, manifested Starfire be Thy hand, Thy breath, Thy will, Thy eyes the thousand suns. Give us this day our needs, and let our wants be Thy domain, and forgive us our unbelief."

We're all silent. I hold my hand up, because I reckon Z's going to say something about blood and honor and probably that it's weak to call upon the blueblood God. "That's a real nice prayer."

"I pray all the time now," Kalia says. "I pray for you guys. I pray for Quinn's soul . . ." And she manages to say his name without her voice cracking. "I'm sorry, Jaqi. This wasn't all your fault."

"You still going to teach me to read?"

"If we survive."

Suits update the coordinates for me, fast as I can follow. We're zipping between the streets with them now, and I got to say, when those metal eyes turn and blaze at us, I can't help feeling like these fellas are hungry. This little ship must look one hell of a snack.

We glide into a hangar in one of them towers. The entrance looms above, about twice as high as the rings of Bill's asteroid. The ribs of the walls are the biggest, blackest pylons you ever seen; little Suit drones scramble over them, like a billion bugs.

The biggest Suits you ever seen pop out of the walls. They were *part* of them pylons, I see now. Black and segmented and long, and they scurry across the metal.

There en't a one of them don't look the image of a centipede.

"Oh, no," I say. I shudder. It had to be worse. It just had to get worse. Maybe this is God's way of talking to me. *En't going to win this one, Jaqi. Just check out the evidence.*

Our ship comes to a stop, and they crowd around us. The biggest, longest of them seems to be dragging himself across the floor. He's got more gear sticking out of them segments than I ever seen—arms with crackling fingers of electricity, pincer hands mounted on crane arms, human hands with too many fingers.

"Time to face them," Z says. He tries to stand and sinks into the seat, and he don't even complain when I grab his arm and help him haul himself to his feet.

"Do we have to?" I say. "Maybe we could just keep going. Jump again. Beyond this."

"There is nothing beyond this," Z says. "Nothing but more Kurguls, more Suits."

"That's my life from now on, en't it?" I say. I mean only Z to hear it, but I guess Kalia does.

She says, "I'm sorry, Jaqi. You'll be able to leave soon. Z can take care of us."

"I en't going anywhere. Not yet."

Our ship's hatchway cracks, and the stink of ozonated air, thick with smoke and the smell of burning wires, leaks in. As the first real planet air I've sniffed since I can't remember, it en't much.

18

Araskar

RASHIYA'S PRACTICE SWORD strikes me right under my ribs. My breath vanishes; red stars explode along my vision. I fall to my knees, on the hard ground of the hangar. At least, from the pain that sings along all my nerves, I'm not numb. That's good, right? I feel my body more keenly than I have in months. Let's throw a damned party.

When I can get my breath back, I mutter, "Good hit. Good match."

"Oh, we're not done," she says. "Got three more nodes until we get around the Dark Zone. We have plenty of time for this. Come at me."

"That an order?"

She raises an eyebrow. "Maybe."

"I used to outrank you, Lieutenant."

"You can take me," she says. "You need to come at me like you mean it."

"I could never take you, you crazing bitch."

"I told you the first night together that you were holding back, and you still are!"

She told me that? I don't remember it. Wonder if that's part of what went into the short soulsword. Yeah, it must be. I can't quite recollect meeting her, now that I put my brain on it.

I suspect that I know why I got rid of that memory.

"I saw you throw your Moth directly into enemy fire. You clung to the burning gun pod. It should have been suicide." She touches the side of my face, and I wince. I didn't realize she had come so close. There's a bruise there too. "Come on. Don't get lost in your head."

"You know me. It's all suicide, I just haven't quite succeeded yet."

"That's not you." She leans in, our faces as close as if we were back in bed, takes my shoulder, doesn't let me pull away. "I need you," she whispers, and I hate how close she's come to my own thoughts.

I look at Rashiya. Really look at her. I imagine her with the original skin on her face instead of that half-melted synthskin leaving fleshy gaps around the circuit in her forehead, without the scar along her jawline. I imagine her without clothes, the ribbons of bruises up her back from training, imagine her laughing.

"Tell me the truth," I say softly. "What's Directive Zero?"

She does that cold, blank stare and pulls away. "That's above your clearance."

"Soldiers gossip," I say.

"Damn right they do." She sighs and pulls back. "Let's not mix orders and fun. Not now. I'll give you a full briefing once this is all over."

I stand there. I hoped she wouldn't do this. I hoped it even when I took that memory.

"Come at me again," she says. "Like you're trying to kill me. Like we're back in the pit for the first time—only now you know what's waiting for you if you're good."

"No," I say. "If I'm trying to kill you, you'll know."

Jaqi

Some things en't meant to be described. You know what's one of them? Sitting in the middle of a nest of black, shining, stinking-of-burn Suits who for some reason *all* have to look like centipedes, only three times bigger, and their coils and legs are skittering around us. Toq holds my hand so hard it hurts. It's a bit of a comfort, really.

Every one of them is divided into metal segments, and each segment sprouts a good assortment of arms, some with organic arms worked into the mix. And old guy . . . there he is, I reckon, the biggest, oldest Suit-a-pede in the room.

He crawls closer. I try not to stop away. Something's odd—*noisy*, I'd say, about this place here. Like there's some kind of interference in the node, bugging out my brain. Maybe it's all them old nodes. Maybe it's all that data.

His voice echoes, not just through the chamber, but in my head. Like they're working so close to the edge that they're on the verge of falling into pure space.

"I'm the Engineer."

This is the Engineer? The biggest and nastiest of all the Suits is Bill's contact? "I'm Jaqi." *The Engineer always honors a bargain.* Better hope Bill wasn't wrong about that.

"I was among the first," he says. "To find the old paths. And you have brought me old data, from before my early days, when the Empire was young."

"You were the first Suit?" I look around at the scrambling hive that is this place. Screens pop up in the middle of the air;

holoscreens projected on nothing, and them reading letters flash across them at near light speed. "You created all this?"

Symbols blur across the screen in front of his face. "Yes, I did."

"Well." I look around, trying to show him that I'm impressed, and not creeped.

"How did you find us?" he asks.

"Bill," I say. "Knows everything."

"What have you brought us?"

I motion for Kalia to come forward. She's clinging to Z's enormous hand as hard as Toq is holding to mine. She's got the black box.

The Suits kind of ripple. I can tell they recognize this thing. "Ancient data," the Engineer says. "The oldest I have seen."

Three twisting, multi-jointed arms emerge from a compartment in the Engineer's chest, reach for it. Kalia shies back. She wants to hang on to the thing, you can tell.

"Give it to us."

"You have to give it back, Engineer," I say.

"We want only the data," the Engineer says. "Your object will be returned when we have read its data."

I reckon there's nothing I can really do to guarantee that. But this is our chance. I hand the thing over to the Engineer.

When I do, something comes through his viewscreen, something that almost could be his face. Circuits and wires and flesh, all mixed up, like a wrinkled, ancient map, with two white, blinking eyes. Then the viewscreen lights up with green letters and numbers. Even if I knew these things, I would be able to follow the way that they flash, faster and faster, across the screen. Must be whole books, whole libraries maybe, that flash across that screen.

The other Suits around are restless, stirring, sending out clicks and creaks. The sight of all that data's got them in a stir.

The little marks keep flashing. "Can you read that?" I ask Kalia.

She shakes her head no. "It's going too fast."

He keeps going like that for a while. I look over at Z. He's swaying on his feet, blinking furiously. He kind of stinks, like there's rot in his body. "You, uh, you guys going to figure this out?"

"It is protected," the Engineer booms. "Ancient code, writ deep. By those who wrote the nodes into the sky."

"Where did you get that thing?" I ask.

"Dad gave it to us," Kalia said.

"Who gave it to him?" Z asks.

Kalia says, "I don't know. Dad liked to collect old things."

The Engineer's scan seems to go on forever. Long enough that I put an arm around Z. "Stay awake," I mutter.

He doesn't answer. He leans on me, and that rot-stink gets stronger. No, this won't do. Maybe if we have the Suits scan him, figure out how to restore him to health. Maybe if we've got something else to bargain with.

And suddenly the Engineer makes a kind of deep, scraping grunt. The red lights in this place dim, and a beam of light erupts from the box, projects itself into the sky over us, and shows—stars.

A star field.

"This is the data?"

"It is a map," the Engineer says.

"Of what?" Those en't any stars I recognize. I've seen the stars of this galaxy from just about every angle, except maybe the way they look from the blueblood worlds.

More of them numbers and letters flash across his screen, a rapid blur of green. "There is no data that tells me," the Engineer says at last. "We have no data on this map."

"That what the old galaxy looks like?" I ask.

"No," Z says, suddenly. He staggers to an upright position, his hand on my shoulder, for all that his hand is three times my shoulder's size. Staring up in wonder, like he's seen a whole standing line of ghosts. "This is the old sky. These are the stars that are now shadowed in the Dark Zone."

"How do you reckon that?"

"Our people remember," he whispers. "There are things too sacred to write. I have it from my father, and my grandfather, and his father and grandfather. That constellation"—he points—"the Great Hunter. My grandmother said that when the Great Hunter went dark, we lost our land, we began the wars against the Empire, and eventually we lost who we truly are." He sounds about ready to break. "I never thought." He looks at me, and his face twists up something strange, even stranger than his half-dead look.

"There is no data for this," the Engineer says.

"I reckon it's because the Empire wiped out this data," I say. "Why do you think we have this?"

Z is still staring at me. "What?"

"It's you," he says, like a whisper.

"Me? The star map is me?"

"You're the one. It's not John Starfire. It's you. 'Who shines a light upon the ancient roads, who leads the people to safety.'"

"The one what?"

Kalia answers, in that same voice she uses for her prayer. "'The son of the stars faces the giants who stride the worlds, and he is armed but by faith.' That's what you mean, Z?"

Z nods his head.

"I en't never heard that."

"It's in the Bible," Kalia says. "The Third Book of Joria."

Z raises a shaky hand. "John Starfire won the galaxy because all crosses believe in that prophecy. But it's not John Starfire. It's Jaqi. And the giants that stride the worlds . . ." He inhales, deep. "No peace will last with the Shir, not so long as they exist to eat suns and prey on life. You are going to bring real peace, lasting peace." His voice breaks a little. "To think that I should die now, when I've seen what my grandfathers waited for."

"Z . . ." You know, I've been telling him for so long that he's been talking crazy, I don't know how to make him listen when he's so obviously out of his head.

"How do you know it's her?" Kalia says.

"Stop encouraging him!" I snap.

"Don't mock me, Jaqi!" Z says, baring teeth. "I know this as I know my father's name."

"I'm pretty sure that prophecy said 'son.' I en't ever been nothing but a daughter."

"There were no words for 'son' or 'daughter' in the old Jorian language," Kalia pipes up, "because the old Jorians didn't have gender. They could change between male and female."

"Really?" Useful, that could be. "I en't going to bring peace and kill the Shir, though."

"You are," Z says. He leans into me. Boy, does he stink. "You destroyed the Vanguard. You saved the children. You will face the Warlord, and you will restore the truth of Joria, and you will . . ." He's struggling for words.

"This is about the most evil crazy thing you've said, and you've said some evil crazy things, Z. I en't no prophecy. Them things are stupid. Religion makes folk crazy. Believing makes folk crazy. Look at the Vanguard. I en't nothing but a girl, a girl who's spent her life smuggling and just wants to have a damn normal life for a little while, and you're making things up when we got enough problems."

"I know, as I know my father's—"

"Let it go, Z!"

He totters away from my shouting face. I grab his arm to keep him steady. I can tell this guy believes in what he's saying. Maybe even Kalia's starting to believe it. Make me want to scream. En't there enough crazing going around?

"Engineer," Kalia says. "Can we access the star map when we want to?"

"I have broken the codes. I can leave it open, thus, but any sentient who can operate this will find the data."

"Hand it back."

He does so, not before another little flash of light across his eyes. "The data is good," he says. Very good." After a moment, he adds, "There is a ship in orbit. They are hailing us. Asking for you."

"Oh."

"They are Vanguard?" Z says.

"They are," the Engineer says.

"How the burning hell did they find us?" I ask. "They couldn't have followed us through the burning Dark Zone!"

Z, leaning on me, mutters, "Good. We will fight them again, and finish them this time, with all the blood and honor of our ancestors, and die in—"

"No, we won't." I look up at old Engineer. "You going to protect us?"

He whirrs a bunch of them gears, deep in his old guts. "We

must make a contract," he finally says, "for protection."

"We gave you well data, you protect us. There's a contract." I point at Z. "While you're at it, find the data on an antidote for him."

"Much more," he says. "It will take much more to protect you." He raises one of them metal tentacle things. "We must take you into ourselves. Your knowledge is great."

It takes me a long, cold-as-space minute to realize he en't talking to me. He's pointing back at Z.

Z bristles. The sweat coating his skin shines in the running lights. "I . . . you want me to become a *Suit*?"

"Your data is precious."

"Wait a moment," I say. "So you could heal him?"

The Engineer holds his peace for a long time, then says, "We do not need his body. We need his data."

For all that Z is near death, he lets out a hell of a snarl. "My ancestors' knowledge is more precious than—" He stops. And for an Imperial minute, his eyes roam over the kids, weighing things. They would be safe here, if anywhere, with Suits all around. Kalia and Toq look back at him, not quite understanding.

I don't know if he even realizes he's speaking aloud. "It would be an honorable death, protecting you. But my people's knowledge, that which must not be written—it cannot be shared. Not like this."

"You en't becoming a Suit, Z," I say. "Look, Engineer, we gave you some serious data. You en't getting Z's brain. You fix him up, in your vats, and you cover our escape." I step forward, ignoring the way he chills my blood.

The Engineer gives a long rumble, and I see that face in there again, that mashed-up bit of flesh and circuitry, older than some planets, I reckon. "We do not heal. You will be protected within our orbit only."

I look between Z and the kids. Kalia grabs Z's hand. "You need to heal him!"

"No," I say, "no, I reckon we can take one more risk." Luck? You there?

19

Jaqi

TWO THINGS.

One: I en't never thought I would have a normal life. I hoped. And hope is a dangerous thing in the wild worlds, as much as nice is. So when they said I was the chosen whatday-athink, the special oogie of space, it confirmed what I'd begun to know was true: I en't getting a normal life, not ever.

It was nice to hope. But right here, leaving atmos from the Suits' mainframe, in Palthaz's old ship, I let go of that hope. Watching the Suit mainframe get smaller below us, a mess of light and blackness, a grid sprawled out across the planet, I let it all go. I en't ever going to be normal.

It hurts, to let go. But what I got en't bad. I got these kids, and I got Z, as long as he hangs on, and for now, we got our lives, if we can survive this.

Second thing: the Engineer gave this rust bucket a bit of a gloss, far as I can tell. It's handling much better than it ought, as we rise into the black of space. It swoops and dives like a dream. He told me about the basic shard-shooter, which Palthaz broke years ago, and has finally been fixed. I can fire off a small enough volley when I need to.

Most importantly, he's stashed parachutes under our seats, and now I tell the kids and Z, "Put 'em on. Only way the

Matakas will leave us alone will be if they see the ship go down." I take a long time wrapping the parachute around me, because I'm making sure that it covers Bill's guitar, strapped to my back in its little bag. "Come on, Z." I wrap the chute around him.

He looks up at me as if he's about to say something—something like *I'm going to die anyway.* I cinch the chute tight around him. "Put it on, Z!"

"You just push this button?" Kalia says, looking at the center of the parachute. "How will I know?"

"Once you're out of the ship, count to five," I say. "You got your black box strapped on?"

She taps it where it's stashed inside her coveralls, taped to her chest. "The Engineer said these are called memory crypts."

"You talked to him?" I say. "More?"

"Just a bit," she says. "He knew a lot. About everything. I asked him whether he thought God was real."

"Did he—" Oh, no time. There's the Vanguard ship. No bug ships yet. And the moon, a long hard shot, fighting gravity from both worlds, beyond it. At least it's a low-orbit, as things go. Had I a bit more time, I could reach it in a few hours.

I don't have hours. I have thrusters pulling fuel from the oxygen stores, to give us a push near the speed of pure space, and a brake just as hard. I've got a small collection of Imperial minutes to get from planet to moon.

"Here we go."

It's simple enough for me. Shoot straight. Right out of atmos, kicking hard right into the blackness, shooting for that moon that's hanging heavy and close, digging into the oxygen stores like you shouldn't in the vacuum. The kids moan as the pressure pushes on them.

Z is rambling. "What cannot be written. I could not give up the things that cannot be written. Blood and honor. I must die in—"

"Not yet, Z," I say. This thing can really move of a sudden; it's just a shame that as soon as we get out of grav, the Vanguard ship starts spitting shells at us, otherwise it'd be one hell of a good ride. "All right, Engineer," I say. As if he can hear me. "Help us out."

Kalia is praying again. "Our Father, who art in Heaven, manifest Starfire be—"

"Keep on praying, girl," I say. "Tell me if that guy hears, too."

The Engineer has done his work well; I hit the buttons and we answer their shard-fire with a volley of our own, and we do some nice ducks and weaves right through the air. Nonetheless, they're closing. Coming to get us. Fast as they know how. Not even bothering with the bugs this time; just trying to get close enough for a tractor beam. That big black ship, sleek and marked with the flame of the Resistance in red against the black metal, moves across the stars.

"Do it, Engineer," I say. What the hell's he waiting for?

Closer. Fast as we're moving, that Vanguard ship is going faster, getting closer, spitting out those shard-bolts, trying to disarm us at least. We're far enough away from atmos now that the ship could blow a hole in us and just do some salvage; maybe they're still shooting to cripple because they want the kids alive.

"Any time, Engineer!" I mutter.

Closer, the Vanguard come.

And there it is.

The yellow cloud streaks across space. Like a nice breath after a good smoke.

The Vanguard, smart as they are, should be able to identify it. Nano-Suits en't unheard of around the galaxy. But the Vanguard are pretty damn focused on us. And so that yellow stream reaches up from the planet and catches the Vanguard ship, even as it pours forth another red volley of shard-fire, across the sky at us. Fingers of yellow creep up the ship. Gobs of red streak from it. Black bits of metal start to break away as the Suits eat the Vanguard ship.

And one of those shard-blasts connects.

We go spinning through space. The ship groans and pops, atmos leaking, suddenly strained for power. Kalia's prayers go higher and screechier. "Our Father!"

"It's okay," I say. It en't, but maybe. "We just need to make the moon. We just need to—"

The ship roars as one of the thrusters burst, blows. We are all thrown forward, our ship hurtling through the darkness. And that's when everything decides to go black for me too, as I'm slammed against the console.

Araskar

The ship's tough to see, with my eyes. The whole planet is lit up, after all, a mass of running yellow and white lights in the darkness, and so one little light rising out of that—who could tell?

I can. My whole soul is burning, alive at the presence of the music that's in her. It's like I took all the pinks in the galaxy. It's all I can do not to walk out the airlock after her. The stirring, sweet notes, the whirl of the strings over the low, pulsing harmony. It visibly pulses around that little baby's-head ship.

"Shoot them," Rashiya commands.

"To cripple," I counter. "Just take out a thruster." Our skeleton crew has rerouted both the links and the weapons to three different stations on the bridge. We've shut off life support to our lower decks and all crammed into one barracks room; with only ten of us left, there's no point. And so a maintenance engineer and a cook deliver the shard-bolts.

"To cripple," Rashiya confirms.

"I'll do my best," says the girl on firing duty.

Rashiya leans forward. "This is it," she says. "I can feel it this time." She looks over at me. "Almost over."

"After this," I say, "we go somewhere far away. Where the rest of the galaxy will never find us."

She doesn't notice how closely I watch her as she laughs. "If only. I have whole years of orders in front of me. Consolidation." She shakes her head.

"Maybe just a bath," I say. Her eyes are still on the screen.

"Now that's crazing talk."

We close in, and one of the shard-bolts catches their thruster. The thruster explodes, throwing what's left of their ship forward, faster and harder along their original destination. "Grab it!" Rashiya says. "Tractor beam. Don't let it get away."

"Yes, ma'am," the command tech says, sounding audibly relieved. "I— What's this?" He looks up at me. "Secondblade, I don't know what these readings mean."

I look at the readings. Confusing. The tractor beam is—is it being rerouted or shut down? "Rashiya, what does this—"

That's when our ship really starts to come apart.

Jaqi

When I get my head up, the moon is much bigger.

Its brown surface fills the screen. The link is squawking; some Matakas are shouting at us. Any minute they'll start shooting too, but no, we're falling so fast we'll burn up as soon as we hit atmos. Too fast. I grab the controls, yank the thrusters. Fire, slow us down, damn it. I fire thrusters like I'm trying to come to a dead stop. Slow us down, just ignore that grav—

The ship is fighting grav, our own inertia, and the thrusters, our three remaining thrusters, are firing and firing. The air in here is getting thinner; I rerouted power to the thrusters just for this quick run so nothing's pumping atmos. Doesn't matter. Doesn't matter that my vision is going black, as long as we can make planetfall. I watch the gauge. We're falling too fast.

Alive. And my chest hurts cuz there en't any air in here. We're falling toward a big empty brown spot in the middle of a continent that's getting closer and closer.

Gravity, real gravity, grabs us and pulls us in. The sky is black, the air is flaming hot, and then, too fast, it's beautiful, bright blue.

"I en't going to die here!" I shout. Didn't even notice I was shouting it.

The ship screams from the pressure of real atmos, metal superheating. The thrusters scream too, fighting gravity to slow up to a safe jumping speed. The pressure fields nearly can't bear it. Z screams, near drowned though he's next to me. His veins are black as his tattoos. He grabs Toq. The fields go, and suddenly all that air, the real live oxygen and carbon dioxide of this moon, slams through our ship.

Z and Toq go flying out the big empty space at what used to be the back of our ship. Into the sky.

I pull the ship up hard, fighting the throttle. Fighting and fighting until—*screech*—the throttle breaks right off in my hand. The shock runs right up my arm. A metal fragment of the throttle pings off the screen, bounces around the cockpit.

I en't never flown in real atmos. Flown plenty in the bigger ecospheres. Flown with lots of tractor beams trying to grab me. But there en't nothing like this. This real grav just wants to eat us.

I hit the autopilot, for whatever it'll do. I jump up, and I grab my pack, grab Kalia, hold her tight and run—just as the side of the ship erupts in flame, the heat screaming a trail across the sky. I jump out of the ship, away from the flame—

Brown below, then blue, and the wind whips us along, falling, always falling toward the desert below.

And pulling at my arms! Kalia is wrenched away out of my grip—I grab her elbow. Her eyes come open, and I yell, "Five!"

The wind pulls her out of my grip. She goes up, up into the blue above me—and her chute opens.

"God!" I shout, and it's about my most devout moment ever, flying through the air, the real air, not vacuum, not ecosphere grit, not canned air but the real thing, then falling, and damn, I have to look down and see that brown desert coming closer and closer before I remember *oh yeah* and I hit the button for my own chute.

It yanks me so hard my eyes go black, but then I'm drifting along in the sky.

In the distance, our ship explodes in a ball of fire over the desert, either from its own disintegrating self or from Mataka fire.

And I sail, through the sweetest air I ever smelled.

Below me, about the most beautiful thing in what must be the entire galaxy. Far as I can see, sand, cut by rough red hills, some of them little more than rocks sticking into the sky, worn away to spires. Scrubby little trees, like black dots. Some big animal is loping across the sand, followed by riders on—are those real horses? Like in the stories?

Wild as the wild worlds come, this moon.

"It's real pretty," I whisper, and my face feels wet. "Real atmos. Real plants." As if in time with the air and the landscape, the guitar strapped close to my back *thrums,* a deep resonant sound.

I'm coming down, too fast, at a pile of high, sharp rocks about the size of them Suit towers. "No, no!" I shout, like that's going to make a difference. I pull my legs up, try to direct myself, and I barely miss the tallest of the rocks, and I'm heading in, toward a wide open space of dirt, but I'm skimming over the ground too fast, my legs scrambling but just moving too fast, and then—

I crash into a sand dune, which is about the only thing that saves me from breaking everything. Sand goes flying everywhere. Sand goes in my eyes, down my throat, up my nose. Scrapes my poor fingers. It burns—it's hot, and it chokes me, dry as space. I gag and fight my way out of the sand and vomit up sand and water and try to wipe sand from my eyes, which only puts more sand in them. Finally I get up, and I can see, bleary, the brown expanse around me, leading to the high rocks I saw before.

I cough and spit out sand. Nice to make your acquaintance, real matter from real earth. Didn't have to come on so strong.

I reach behind me, feel the guitar. Feels like it's still in one piece. I drop the parachute and, on legs that are still throbbing in pain, I stumble across the openness toward the rocks. Maybe some water over there. They got water all over the place on these real planets. No need to go get your recycled liquid depot. Real water, better than comet-stuff, and I can just stick my head in one of them big rivers folks talk about and wash all this sand off—

A loud boom echoes through the atmosphere.

I look up. My eyes en't so good, full of sand, but I can see it. I recognize the shape, even from here.

It's a pod from that Vanguard ship.

20

Araskar

THE POD RATTLES and we lurch along through the atmos. Kurguls are shouting in our comlink, no doubt ready to come shoot us down, but this is one empty, nasty, waterless, and Godforsaken piece of desert moon, and I don't think they'll find us before we find our quarry. We can deal with Kurguls, even Matakas. Too bad we couldn't deal with microscopic Suits.

Even after the chutes deploy, our pod lands hard, skidding across sand and rolling, and we are out as soon as it quits shaking.

Rashiya exhales. "I've got the reading on the memory crypt." She runs her hands along the circuits in her forehead. "This is almost over. Almost over." She looks up into the sky. "I hope the other pods made it. Between Matakas and the Suits . . ."

"Let's finish the mission," I say.

My hand isn't shaking, I notice. It feels nice and calm on the soulsword's hilt. I hope the crew made it, too. I hope there aren't any more needless deaths today.

Stupid hope.

Ridges of weathered stone reach to the sky, higher and more varied than towers in any city, run between empty, sandy stretches. The only trees are small, scrubby things clinging to the slopes of the rock. In the sky, the Suits' world is just visible as an impression, a huge dark crescent. It's beautiful, in a desolate kind of way, and as the first naturally occurring atmos I've breathed since Irithessa, it goes right to my head, rushes into my blood. It even kills the headache that I've had since I tossed the pinks.

We are close to a curved rock shaped like a sword; a high weathered red thing stretching into the sky. Reminds me of something, though I can't say what.

"The human girl is just over here," Rashiya says. She trudges off into the sand. I follow her.

In the shadows of that curved rock, a figure crawls along on hands and knees, dragging the weight of a parachute behind her. She looks up at us, myself, and Rashiya. I catch up with Rashiya, stand next to her.

This is the human girl, then. Formoz of Keil's daughter, keeper of our much-desired intel. About ten years old, face bruised and streaked with dirt and lips trembling. Sand has crusted on her eyelashes and is thick in her hair. She's praying, I realize. Probably has been praying for weeks.

And here is what my slugs died for, what that ash pile was for: a crying little girl at the end of the wild worlds.

"Give it to me," Rashiya says to the little girl. "Give me the memory crypt."

"Father in Heaven, Father . . ."

"The black box. Give it to me." Rashiya draws her soulsword, a loud, ringing song of steel in the empty desert air. It shines black, radiating heat.

I draw my own sword.

The girl gets up, on her knees, still babbling.

"I won't hurt you. Just give it to me. You came this far, and there is nothing else you can do to get away. To resist me would be very stupid, and would get you killed, like your brother, and you want to live." Rashiya leans forward.

The girl finally stops praying long enough to untangle the parachute straps. She reaches inside the dirty coveralls she's wearing and pulls out a little box.

Rashiya snatches it up. "Good." She looks over it. Looks just like a black box, unless you look closely and see the tiny curves of Jorian writing. She visibly slumps in relief. "Devil take me, I thought I'd never finish this mission."

"What's it say?" I ask the girl.

Rashiya perks up, looking between me and the girl.

"What does this thing tell about?" I ask. "I know it's a memory crypt. What did it tell you?"

The little girl's face contorts, bits of sand falling away from it. "You murdered my brother!" She clutches at the sand. "I won't tell you anything!"

I cut my hand with the soulsword, let the fire spring up. "Tell me," I say. "Your other brother and your friend are still close enough for us to find."

And as she meets my eyes, I wonder if I look any different than Rashiya did, when she killed the girl's brother. Probably not. Probably I look worse, with my scars and my slurring voice and the blood trailing off my fingers. The girl begins to cry. "It's . . . it's a star map. It's a star map, of what the Dark Zone used to be. Oh, God, don't hurt my little brother! Don't hurt Jaqi!"

Rashiya takes a minute, then whispers to me. "Araskar, if what she said is true, we can't leave her alive. We can't risk anyone knowing. I'm sorry, but . . ."

I close my eyes and I bring the faces to my head. It's not hard. My dead friends, my slugs, my batch mates, were all cut from the same fifteen models, so for all that I have a thousand ghosts haunting me, they all have the same faces.

I turn to Rashiya. "We can't leave any humans alive, you mean."

She doesn't seem surprised. She just sighs. "Soldiers gossip, ai?"

"I figured it out." I hold my soulsword up to her. "I didn't sign on for genocide, Rashiya. Neither did my slugs."

She holds up her hands. "Fine. We won't kill kids. I have the box, we've got the intel, no one else needs to know."

It would be so easy. If I just nod, then we could get back to the pod, and then threaten the Matakas with Vanguard so they give us a ship, and we could even say that the kids are dead, killed in planetfall. We could go back to Irithessa and pass on the intel, and I could finally ask for reassignment, far from the battlefield, where I can just not think about what the Resistance is really doing, what "consolidation" really means, and I can go back to the pinks and no one will care, sit with the music and not care that John Starfire himself, the Chosen One, is mocking what my friends died for.

"Araskar," she says. "Let's go."

"I'm not going."

"Oh?"

"You have two choices, Lieutenant," I say, and I summon those fifteen faces. "You can tell me exactly why your pater's keen to kill half the galaxy. Or I can find it out for myself, with this."

"I said let's go, soldier."

"I'm not your soldier anymore." I slide into a ready position,

188 • Spencer Ellsworth

my soulsword ready to catch the blows from hers. "Consider this my resignation."

She lunges. I counter her stab, sling her sword away. She turns, and she's back at me, beating at my strokes, her sword too fast, too quick, as I hammer her blows away. I go backward, across the dirt, up the scrubby, rocky slope.

She's going to kill me. We played this through practice, and each time, her practice sword struck my breastbone, my solar plexus, my neck. I'm catching and deflecting a few blows. Our hilts lock and I run back, she stabs and I parry to the side, and then her next blow slashes open my arm, and I catch another blow at the hilt but it pierces my side, rips a hole.

"Araskar!" She dances back from my pathetic thrust. "Don't make me do this!"

My blood runs down the hilt onto the blade of my soulsword. It glows with white fire, shining even in the desert's afternoon heat. I parry her next blow, try my own stab, but she's so damn fast.

She backs up, inviting me forward. "You know we have orders—"

I throw myself into a downhill lunge. She catches it. Faster than she should, she throws my blade off and her own blade strikes at my neck. I twist, turn away, but it slices deep into my shoulder and blood coats my sword arm and I drop my soulsword, stumble and fall on my face into the dust. I try to get up, on my good arm. I fall again.

She kicks me. As she stands over me, I see both that hate and that sorrow in her eyes. "I have a mission," she whispers. She puts her boot at my throat. "You know I have to finish it."

And then she is walking away. Holding her soulsword high. About to kill the little girl.

I will not let this happen.

The music swells inside me, a feverish living roar. I get to my feet and grab my soulsword in my bad left hand and I charge and she turns and she looks genuinely, awfully surprised as I shove the blade through her chest.

"Araskar, I—" She can't say any more, not through the metal in her airway.

"I'm sorry," I say, and feel totally stupid. "I'm sorry."

She coughs, gags out a few words. "Pull it out. Don't do—"

I don't pull it out.

My soulsword sucks up Rashiya like a thirsty man at a tin of cold, clear water.

I see everything. I listen as her father talks, as he tells her everything from how to consolidate the galaxy to this missing memory crypt to the way he shivers at night and babbles about all his enemies, still trying to find him, his voice a high, pitter-pattering pathetic mad thing, whispering of the enemies he's had for so long.

I know her father's secret. The reason why he wants to kill every last blueblood.

He knows what the Shir are.

He knows that any peace with the Shir means that he must give them more to eat. The bluebloods knew it too, and he fears that any human will know.

She believes him. Why shouldn't she? She can't see his paranoia, his madness, without thinking of all the times he's been proven right.

She fights as I did, in the bloody hallways of the Imperial Navy. She kills the loyal crosses of the Imperial forces, throws her grenades, fires her shard-bolts. She thinks of her father, and her mother, and it gives her strength. She thinks of what they told her: she is a new generation, the first of the new Jorians, born of crosses who broke free. They can't live without a galaxy purged. They can't become as the ancients unless humans are gone.

She believes. And she loves. She loved me, as strange as that was. I can see myself, as I looked through her eyes. I looked like the hero her father said I was. I also look like someone else under a burden of destiny and expectation, same as she was. Huh. Never thought of myself that way.

She thinks she knows who betrayed the Resistance. I reach for the hunch, the suspicion, which she has buried . . .

She's dead. Her body has gone cold and empty on the end of the soulsword.

I lay her down in the sand and draw the soulsword out of her chest. There is no blood. The white fire along the soulsword has died down. Her eyes look up at me, still locked in that strange mixture of admiration and horror.

I lay her down. I stroke her hair. She was the last one, from my very first battalion. Every single one of us, except crazing me, is now dead. "Stamp your boots and open your sheath."

The Resistance might suffer for it, but I know it now, from her memories: John Starfire conquered the galaxy and brokered a peace with the Shir. He also became a paranoid, weak man.

Hell, I can't blame him. War does funny things to us. I brush my hand over the ripples where her synthskin melted. War takes away pieces of everyone.

I unsheathe the short sword. It gleams in the sun. This time, it'll take away every single one of my bloody memories. Along with my bloody life.

Jaqi

I just now begin to remember something from those stories about deserts: there en't much water in them. Huh. That's the kind of thing a girl should remember.

I stumble along, just noticing how hot it is—a different, open, drying-out heat from Swiney Niney. A mixture of that sweaty, nasty Swiney heat with the dryness of Bill's place when it was over-vented. Way too dry. Like the humidity control's off. Not bad, though. Air is sure sweeter than any reverse-cell crap I've ever tasted.

It takes forever to reach the nearest spires of rock. Everything is far apart here. Never seen this much open space that I can remember. I get myself up and over the hill, and down the other side and . . .

Kalia, running. She's not hurt, although she's absorbed half a planet's worth of dirt on her skin and her clothes. "Jaqi!" She looks up at me, mouth open. "They—they—Vanguard!"

I run with her, into the shadow of the biggest rock.

It en't the scene that I expected. I recognize gray girl, what killed Quinn. She's lying on the ground, and she's dead, that weird ghostly pale look that means she's been stuck with a soulsword. The other guy I think I recognize too. Scar-face. Wait, I saw this fellow, inside one of the Moths, when he humped my ship! Couldn't reckon how I saw him, but I know that face.

He is kneeling on the ground, and has a short sword out, and his hand is trembling, holding it at his chest.

"He killed her." Kalia is silent except for her quick, panting breaths. "He killed her and then . . . then he just kneeled down."

I take a good look. He's all bloody, with a wound in the meat of his shoulder and another in his side. Short sword, at the ribs. He's going to do himself in, one of them honor things that are so important to the rest of the galaxy.

I don't say anything. Let the bastard off himself. It don't matter whether he saved Kalia; he didn't save Bill, or Quinn, or any of gray girl's other victims. The last few days of running, bleeding, bruises and pain and jumping from node to node, losing friends and changing too fast, bolt through my head, the pain shoved into me like a ship being pulled into a node.

Let him die, I think. It'll help balance out the universe.

"Hey, stop," Kalia says. She runs forward, pushing for the guy. "Stop! You saved my life, you don't have to die!"

He looks up, and he sees me. Something passes between us, a shock through the inside of my bones. I find myself saying, "Enough people have died already."

Crazing enough, I mean it.

He takes that knife away from his chest.

21

Jaqi

HE JUST KEEPS LOOKING at me, his scarred lips open a bit, his brows creased in a way that squashes that scar along the side of his eye.

"What the burning Dark are you looking at?"

He says it real flat, deadpan. "You're unusual."

"I've heard."

He remains on his knees. That shaking hand holds the short blade, but at least it's fallen down a bit, to his side, where it can't bring any more blood to this bloody, bloody day. I sit down on the ground. I could use some water about now, aiya. Evil I could. "Kalia, have you seen Toq and Z?"

"I haven't," she says.

"We'd better find them." I look on the Vanguard fellow. "You staying here? I need help finding our crew." I finger the pistol at my hip, hoping he doesn't notice that it's empty. "Or have you decided which side you're on?"

He stands up, groaning, holding his bloody side. "Go ahead," he says. His voice slurs like he's half cooked. "I'll follow."

I keep looking over my shoulder at him as we start off through the sand. He is holding that little sword and staring at it. I look at him so much that I don't even notice when Kalia screams.

Z is lying, all tangled in his chute, in the middle of the sand, not too far from where Kalia came down. Lying dead still, his skin now a distinct shade of green. As we get closer, I smell that faint rot. No.

Kalia runs to him. She grabs at her waist, pulls out a small flask of water—good thinking, Kalia—and splashes it across Z's face. The water runs in the hollows around his eyes, past his nose and down, and over his lips. The sunlight makes it look like little jewels, scattered across his face. He don't move.

"He's not dead," Kalia says. "He can't . . ."

"Dead, like he wanted," I say. In blood and honor. Except—no, damn it, that Necro-Thing was already dead, and as he said, there's no honor in fighting it, and so there en't no honor in being killed by its poison. Only honor in protecting a couple of kids, far above and beyond what was asked of him. Only honor in being the bravest bastard ever flew the galaxy.

"Z." I lean over and grab his shoulders. "Z, no! Come on! You been poisoned before! Not enough blood and honor! Not enough—" There's something raw and horrid taking up my throat, like all the crying I want to do is finally going to rocket out and I won't be able to stop crying for years.

He puts his hand on my shoulder. Scar-faced Vanguard, and he's holding out his soulsword. Like I ought to take it. "Here," he says.

"What?" He's holding out that stupid long sword, still flickering with white fire.

"There's . . . there's an old story." He rolls his eyes. "I am stupid even for saying it, but there's something different about you." I want to tell him he en't making sense, then give him the punch he deserves, but he clears his throat. "The original Jorians supposedly could heal with their soulswords as well as kill. I believe you can touch the Starfire, perform the miracles, like the original Jorians could."

I wipe at my eyes. "Crazing bastard."

"Probably." He motions with the sword. "Worth a try."

"I en't a cross like you, idiot," I say. It's this guy's damn fault, all of it, anyway, and it's all I can do to keep from choking him, and then smashing his stupid Vanguard helmet with a brick.

He surprises me. "You are more than I am," he says softly. "You have to be, or nothing was worth it. Please. Put your hand with mine, on the sword."

More than . . . Whatever, it's worth a shot. "What do we do?"

"Think of . . ." Long silence, and I reckon he's looking for some way to explain some magical, Starfire-bending, space-twisting spell of the Vanguard to me. "Think of a song."

"What?"

"A song. Do you know any songs?"

I almost laugh, it's so dumb. "You want me to sing while we do this?"

"I don't want you to sing. I want you to think of a song. Just—think about music." He grimaces. "You know the moment when you first hear music? When you first begin to lose yourself in a piece of music? Like that."

The only songs I can think of are Bill's old dirty ones, and I open my mouth to say it—no, that en't all. Maybe it's something about the planetside air, but I think of my mother's voice. Singing something softly, some bit of farmer song, a soft rhythm that went *bend, bend, bend your back. Pull, pull, pull, pull the weed. Bend, bend, bend your back.* In my memory, she sings it soft and gentle, lulling me to sleep.

I realize he's pushed the sword down. Put the tip into Z's chest, right into the big, black-oozing welt that the NecroWasp's stinger made. The white fire ripples along that sword. I hold on. The thing is hot and alive, like holding on to a shard-bolt.

I feel something inside myself. A knot of fire myself, a knot of everything—that anger, over everyone lost, but also the love for my parents, gone as they are, the love for Bill, and the love for Kalia and Toq and even Z, the big scab.

And I hear—I hear something.

It's my mother's voice this time, for real. Singing her farm-worker's song. *Pull, bend, pull, bend.* But there's music with her, music like I en't ever imagined. Soft and gentle little notes ping-pong across this wide space behind her voice. And then they change, become this countersong, this thing made of vast spaces, filling up her words, sharp walls of high and sudden notes, deep thrumming waves of low notes, and I know this. This en't just hopping into a node. This is the Starfire itself. The song of the stars. This is what them Jorians always talked about, and it's sweet, like something that was right there, but I couldn't feel it all along. I en't never heard music like this. En't nobody heard music like this.

"Push," he says. "Push it out, into him."

I reach into that music. The beats go round and round, swirling around me, and I don't push them so much as direct them, make them hold together in a stream, down through the soulsword. The song of the stars, shoving it down into Z.

He gasps for air.

The Vanguard takes the sword out.

Z sits up, feels his chest, and though the welt's still there, it's just a nasty scar now, not a hole through his chest. His skin is pale white under the tattoos. Not a sign of green.

"I—I died."

"Not enough blood and honor," I say, and it's hard to talk around that big thing in my throat. "Had to bring you back."

"Where is Toq?" He stands up and looks around.

I stand up too. In the distance, I can hear something coming. Not a ship. Weird noise. Steady beats, like feet, pounding fast as a ship across the earth.

"Matakas?" I ask. "At least maybe they have some water." I look over at Vanguard. "What's your name, crazing?"

"Araskar," he says.

We wait. Three folks are coming toward us—on real horses! I en't never seen a real horse before. Of course, I en't brought no one back from the dead either. It's a day full of new things.

They stop, a good thirty paces away. They're all wrapped up in white rags, across their faces, just showing the edges of their eyes. They got these funny little decorations everywhere—on strings, like beads. Made of real matter, too, far as I can tell. I've never seen beads made of rocks and wood and bone.

These are no Matakas. Reckon it makes sense that Matakas wouldn't be the only things on this whole moon, that maybe some scabs are running around the desert, just trying to get by. Or running interference for Matakas.

Well, gray girl's gone, and this Vanguard seems to be on my side. And hell, I just brought my friend back from death. En't scared to talk to new folk after that.

One of them rides forward on that horse.

Maybe it's my head, but this horse is about the most beautiful thing I've ever seen. It's taller than Z, and it's got these long, knobby legs that just kind of trot in this way I en't never seen before, just taking giant-size strides like they en't nothing, one stride and another. It looks at me long enough, them black eyes shining, that I suspect this thing is probably sentient.

Z is still on the ground, trying to rise on his arms, looking mighty weak. And that horse comes nearly up to him. The rider reaches up, pulls off that veil. He—no, *she*, she's got white skin, covered with those black, interlacing tattoos; she's another Zarra. I reckon she's going to say *blood and honor*, just to finish this day off right.

Instead, she says, "We have water, and food. We found the boy. He is all right." She looks over us all. "Do the Kurguls know you are here?"

"I think, as far as they reckon, we've been shot down."

"Good." She puts a hand out to Z. He rises, and clasps her hand. "We are many, all who have run."

Araskar

The girl—Jaqi, her name is—and the children, Toq and Kalia, and that enormous Zarra, are all sitting around the fire with our new hosts.

I watch. The people here are a mix of races. Zarra. Rorgs. Tall, bony, thin-faced, fanged Grevans. Keekuks, the "crickets," on their segmented, springing legs. And even a few humans. Skin, scales, hollow eyes, and ridges on the head are lit up by the fire, playing unique shadows across each face, soft round flesh, and dagger-sharp angles, but each face looks on Jaqi and the kids with wonder. They've all run here, to the end of the universe, barely subsisting in this harsh place. No doubt the young Matakas get drunk and come out here to take potshots at them, and they count it worthwhile for the isolation. The Suits might even try to raid them, when they need organic matter. They've all run here, though, to survive, and as Jaqi and the kids tell their story, casting wary glances my way, their noises of assent in various tongues go around the circle.

A good place to run to.

I wish I could forget that I didn't run here.

I slip away from the fire.

I walk out into the desert. It only takes a few steps and the heat from the fire vanishes; I go cold all over, my skin prickling. My wounds ache under the emergency gel-packs used to seal them. The air smells big and bitter cold, like it's carrying all the emptiness of the wild worlds.

My hand goes to the short soulsword's hilt.

Rashiya's memories are still roiling inside me. When you're a cross, you don't put much value on your life, and I can't stop living through her memories of me, because, more fool her, she put value on mine. She may have been Daddy's girl, but when she joined, she cut off all contact with him, didn't let him know where she was. She was one of us, for a while. She trusted our battalion, loved us, lost her friends in the same way I did, and came to me as if we really were from the same batch.

She shouldn't have saved me on Irithessa. Would have done us all a lot of good if those Kurguls got me in the head. Imagine how simple things would be now.

I draw the soulsword and flip it over. It reflects the bright Suit planet that takes up half the sky. Can't help wondering, now, which memory I put in there. I haven't searched my memories closely enough to figure out what's missing.

"You really committed to this grim?"

I can hear the music around her, and I turn around, stare.

The girl is a fountain of the music. The music is staggering in its complexity, and beautiful in its simplicity, in the way a simple tune rises above a gulf of sound.

"You really want to die?"

I hold up the blade, but don't bother to speak. She's right. Right as hell. I really want to die. It's not fair that all my friends, all my slugs, are dead, and here I try to do the right thing and keep living for it.

"Araskar," she says. Speaks my name. "You got some well things to live for—look at them kids. You saved them. You know we have some big secret? You ought to see it—it's a star map, real old, from the time of the first Jorians themselves—and don't think we en't grateful, cuz I know you risked a lot to do what's right."

I have no answer for her. "That star map would be something to see," I settle on. I look out at the stars, beyond the Suits' wide world, the Dark Zone just rising, a black patch beyond the white rim of the mainframe planet.

"There's more to do," she says. "I saw this star map, and they said it was some prophecy, and started rattling on about the Dark Zone. You're one of them Vanguard—what do you know about that?"

"The Third Book of Joria?"

"I reckon."

"I'm not much of a reader," I say. I think of old John Starfire, babbling about it. I wonder whether he's ever truly believed that he is that man in the prophecy. "I know people believe it."

"Right, I reckon so, reckon it's evil crazed. Between you Vanguard, Kalia's praying all the time, and Z's business about blood and honor, I want no religion." She sits down in the sand, not far from me.

"The prophecy might be nonsense, but . . ." The knowledge filters in, the secrets Rashiya's father was trying to keep. "John Starfire made peace with the Shir by promising them more to eat. It was a trade-off. For years the Shir have fought the Navy, and it's kept the Dark Zone from expanding. John Starfire had to pay a price. He promised them . . ." The words trickle into my head. "He promised them they could expand into the wild worlds."

"More of the devils?" She shudders. "He wants to let them go?"

"He wants to control the galaxy and get rid of any challengers," I say. "For now, the Shir don't matter to him, because they're a threat he'll take on later, once he creates a Third Empire." So far she hasn't commented on my slur. I like this girl.

"You know what them Shir are?" she asks. "You find that out in your . . . studies?"

"No," I say. John Starfire knows, but he didn't tell Rashiya. Evolved life? Sentient, even? "They eat life. Planets, stars, people. The Empire wasn't interested in studying them, just keeping them contained."

She says, "We jumped into that Dark Zone. I saw one of them. It was . . . evil scary, and it was hungry."

"Billions of people will die, at least," I say. "He'll get his Third Empire, though. Until he can't control the Shir anymore."

"What the hell do you want to die for when you might be able to stop that?" she says. "Seems to me like you spent all that time soldiering for a crazing fool, you might have amends to make."

I find myself turning on her. "Don't you slight the Resistance. We gave everything to free little dodgers like you." I stop myself from saying *You should have been there with us, if you care about a cross's rights.*

"Then why've you all gone crazing?"

"Not all." She looks at me like I'm some kind of idiot. "I didn't know everything that John Starfire wanted to do. And not everyone does. There will still be good crosses in the Resistance, who are willing to help for the cause of real justice. There are many who believe."

"That's why we gotta fight, scab!"

"And if we could make them think that John Starfire isn't the one in the prophecy, maybe—"

"I en't the prophecy girl," she says, cutting me off. "Can't be. Not me. I'd be late to save the universe, or show up drunk, or some other damn thing."

This girl is, other than her other strange qualities, a snappy one. "Your followers will believe, and you need to act like you are the one, whether you are or not."

How about that? Here I am, using John Starfire's words against him.

She stares up at Trace like it's about to fall on her. "I en't the one," she mutters. "Crazing fools, all of you. Anyway, slab, we have a star map for what used to be the Dark Zone. Maybe the Suits or someone can figure out what used to be there, and where them Shir came from. You figure out where they're from, and then you call some of your friends in the Resistance who might key in, and . . ." She frowns. "What's it called when you have a resistance to a Resistance?"

"Counter-resistance?"

She frowns. "En't there a fancier word for that?"

"Resisting Resistance?"

"Better keep that mouth shut, slab, if that's what comes out."

"Why don't you think of something better?" I look long at her. The planet's light is catching her face, faintly, a faint gleam off her nearly black skin. "You have hope," I say softly.

"En't got anything else," she says. "Might as well keep hope. Here. You play?"

It's then that I notice the guitar she's brought. It sits on the sand next to her, catching the light.

"No, I don't play," I say.

"Learn," she says, handing it to me. "I en't got time, what with that kid wanting to teach me to read. We're going to need some music on this trip, and you always talking about it." She reaches over, and hesitates. And finally, she touches the scar on my face. "It was hard to go against your friends, aiya?"

I swallow, my synthskin tongue twitching. "Yes."

I look at the guitar long after she leaves. Is this what hope looks like? Just wood and string, but full of unreleased notes, unembodied songs, whole soaring suites that I need to learn to play.

Jaqi

Odd scab, that guy. I kind of still want to punch him, but I figure I've got to forgive and let it go; he saved all of us and made himself a traitor to the most powerful folk in the galaxy, and he knows how to swing that blade.

I walk back into the circle, around the fire. The kids are asleep, on Z's shoulders. Everyone else, our new friends, talking quietly. Variety of languages. I know some of them—I reckon I know more languages than Kalia, which is nice to think, given she knows just about everything in them books.

I don't let myself look too long at Z, or think about earlier today, and what I just did. It's going to be some time before my evil small brain can think on that one. I brought a big old slab back from the dead. That's evil good news, except that it makes me just what he said I was.

No, let's think of that tomorrow. I sit back down.

"Here," says one of the tribesmen, a fella with a bone mask pulled up over his scaly face, showing only his little yellow eyes.

"Here what?"

"Food," he says. "From the gardens. You have come a long way, and we offer you something precious."

"You fed us plenty of that horse meat, and it was sure better than a protein—" I catch my breath at what he's got.

"This is precious. To welcome you."

He's got something in his hand. He drops it in mine. Firm, but yielding. The firelight catches the smooth skin, and I turn it over.

I may have lost that normal life, but the universe finally did me a kindness.

It's a tomato.

———————

To be continued in
The Starfire Trilogy: Book Two
Shadow Sun Seven

Acknowledgments

Massive thanks to my amazing editor, Beth Meacham. I think every writer thanks their editor for "taking a chance on this manuscript," but in this case it's more apt than ever, folks, because the first draft Beth saw was ROUGH, and she saw something worth smoothing. Huge thanks to everyone at Tor.com who helped midwife the Starfire Trilogy and get the word out, and to Sparth for the awesome cover. Thanks to the super-agent Sara Megibow, who is always there for every question, and always fighting to get the book into the hands of readers. Not just agent. Super-agent.

Huge thanks as well to Cascade Writers, the best damn writing workshop in the world, that introduced me to said agent and editor.

A very special lumbering two-ton mammoth of THANK-YOU to Langley Hyde, who has been the number one beta reader and number one idea bouncer for Starfire, always coming up with ways to BIGGERIFY the story. You probably deserve a cowriting credit, but for now I hope you'll settle for a latte and a muffin on Sunday morning.

Special credit to my dad, who read just about every story from Super Tiger to this one, and cheered them all on. Thanks, Pop. Thanks also to my sisters, brothers and my mother for the stories they've read and the encouragement they've given me over twenty years. Finally, all credit goes to Chrissy, Adia, Sam & Brigitta. Your love fuels every word.

About the Author

Photograph by Chrissy Ellsworth

SPENCER ELLSWORTH's short fiction has previously appeared in *Lightspeed, The Magazine of Fantasy & Science Fiction,* and *Tor.com.* He lives in the Pacific Northwest with his wife and three children, works as a teacher/administrator at a small tribal college on a Native American reservation, and blogs at spencerellsworth.com.

TOR · COM

Science fiction. Fantasy. The universe.

And related subjects.

*

More than just a publisher's website, *Tor.com* is a venue for **original fiction, comics,** and **discussion** of the entire field of SF and fantasy, in all media and from all sources. Visit our site today—and join the conversation yourself.

CPSIA information can be obtained
at www.ICGtesting.com
Printed in the USA
LVOW12s2325081017
551717LV00001B/80/P